Fables, Fictions and Fantasies: A Compendium

Chloe Cocking

Filidh Publishing

Copyright 2018 Chloe Cocking

ISBN 978-1-927848-37-1
First Soft Cover Edition
Filidh Publishing, Victoria, British Columbia

Cover Design by Danny Weeds
Front cover photo credit: Tim @ Photovisions
(Tim Vrtiska)
Back cover photo credit:
Siska Vrijburg on Unsplash

Other books by Chloe Cocking:
Blood Rain (2018)

For Rob, again and always.

Table of Contents

Schiffman's Asthmador	1
Tight as a Nostril	13
Hair of the Dog	17
Janice's Secret: A *Blood Rain* prequel	34
The Deli Cat	41
My Books Have Disappeared!	48
Thirty-five Arrested in Riot at Vegan Strip Club	59
Where Did This Box Come From?	77
Feed Me	83
The Drunk Parrot: A Modern Fable	89
Do You Want the Head?	103
Irresistible: A *Blood Rain* prequel	108
Bettina's Birthday	124

Schiffman's Asthmador

Missouri, 1938

As the sun was setting, Chet leaned against the chain link fence across the road from the prison's driveway. He looked cool and confident, except for the twitchiness of his hands, and a certain haunted look in his brown eyes.

Should he have a smoke while he waited to catch Johnston, the prison screw, as Johnston headed home for the day? Smoking always calmed Chet's nerves.

When he was inside, he'd seen that Johnston could be relied on to procure a little reefer, or a Valomilk candy bar, or some French postcards for the prisoners—for the right price, of course.

He had heard rumours Johnston might do more than bring in contraband. Quite a bit more, according to some of the hard-timers on Chet's cell block. He believed them. He wanted something very particular, and Johnston was the only one who could help.

He felt his chest tighten as he waited. He noticed he was wringing his hands. *Better calm down.* Being nervous sometimes brought on one of his asthma attacks. *No time for that now.* He reached into his pocket for his smokes. He admired the new packaging—before he'd gone into the joint, Schiffman's Asthmador cigarettes had come in plain grey cardboard boxes by prescription. Now, two years later, you could buy them off the druggist's shelves. The new packaging was eye-catching—a tin case enameled Kelly green with a drawing of some chump, presumably Schiffman himself. Chet reckoned he'd seen better heads on mugs of beer.

He placed the medicated cigarette between his lips, closed the shiny case with a satisfying *snick*, and struck a match against the sole of his prison-issue work-boots. He'd only been out of the joint for a couple of days, and wasn't interested in shopping for new shoes. So far the only thing he'd bought were a few tins of Asthmador. He had smoked two entire tins in the last two days, and was half-way through his third. Chet loved the things. He hadn't been able to get them very often when he was in the joint, mainly because Doucette took everything—food, clothes, self-respect—and beat him to a paste if him tried to object. Chet learned fast and took his lumps. What else could he do?

It was full dark now. *Where the hell was Johnston?* Chet stamped his feet to warm them up. A '37 Ford emerged from the prison's gravel driveway, headlamps piercing the dark. *This is it!* Chet flagged the car down. Sure enough, Johnston was at the wheel, heading home after shift change.

"Heya sissy, miss your prison boyfriend?" Johnston's neck was thicker than Chet's bicep. Even after working a ten in the prison, his uniform was clean and pressed; he kept his hair cut short and neat, his face clean-shaven. Despite all that, something about Johnston made Chet want to wash his hands.

Chet's brows met in a frown, but he kept his cool, shrugged off his discomfort. "Gimme a ride, Johnston, I can make it worth your while."

Johnston looked him up and down, then leaned across the bench seat and opened the passenger side door. Chet flicked the butt of his smoke on the ground and got in the car.

Johnston drove for a quarter mile, and when Chet didn't speak, eventually Johnston did.

"Ok, Nancy, what do you need?"

He took a deep breath, steadying his nerves. "I want Doucette's head in a fucking box."

Johnston smirked, but it melted from his face when he saw that Chet was serious.

"Didn't like being the little woman for your cellie?"

"Exactly."

"What makes you think I'm the man for the job?"

Chet smiled and pulled his wool jacket closer around his wiry form. He drummed his fingers on the tin Asthmador case in his pocket. "People talk in prison."

"So?"

"This car proves it. How do you have last year's model on a prison guard salary?"

Johnston grinned, macabre in sudden boyishness. "Would you believe my wife is an heiress?" He winked.

Chet shuddered inwardly, but kept his cool. "I would not. Look at you: you're an animal."

Johnston stopped smiling. He thought a beat. Then he said, "Head actually sawed off and delivered in what, a wooden butter box?"

"Yep."

"No fooling, cut it off? Not just give him a Cinncinati smile?

"If I wanted his throat slit, I coulda done that myself."

"Sure, right," Johnston sneered.

Johnston drove on in silence.

"Five hundred," he said.

A fortune, to be sure, but Chet knew where he could get his hands on that kind of scratch. Even though he was poor, his grandfather was not. The old man didn't believe in banks or paper money. He always converted any money not needed for immediate expenses into gold coins or gems and kept the whole stash squirrelled away in his house. If you asked him about it, Gramps would tell you a long and boring story about how his own father lost his fortune when Confederate bills became worthless after the Civil War.

The old man had still been sharp when Chet went into prison, but according to a letter Chet's sister sent him about six months ago, Gramps had changed. He was so addled now, he wouldn't notice if Chet helped himself to all the little stashes the old man had hidden over the years.

"Five hundred in gold coins and gems ok with you?" Chet asked.

"Gold coins yes, gems no. Too easy for them to be glass or paste or something. Hard to get value out of them from pawn shops and fences. When do you want it done?"

"By tomorrow night."

"Tight time frame. Better make it six hundred."

"Sure," Chet said, taking the green enamel tin from his pocket, "Mind if I smoke?"

"Do your worst, Tiger. And I want half up front, the other half on delivery."

Chet gave Johnston his grandfather's address, and shortly they pulled up out front. Johnston turned off the engine.

"House don't look like much, you sure you got that money?" Johnston said. He cracked his knuckles against the steering wheel.

"Three hundred up front, three hundred when you bring me Doucette's head in a box. I'll be back in twenty minutes with the first payment, wait here."

Johnston shrugged. Chet exited the car and used his key to open his grandfather's front door. The old man was sprawled on the chesterfield, jaw slack as he slept. The arm of the chesterfield was damp from Gramps' drooling. The radio was on full blast, tuned to some comedy programme Chet had never heard before. Lots of changes in the past two years.

Chet walked quietly through his grandfather's house, searching all the niches and hiding places he had discovered when he was a boy. It took only ten minutes to find slightly more than three hundred dollars' worth of gold coins.

He carefully counted the gold coins. *I can come back tomorrow night to find the rest*. He put what he needed to give to Johnston into a pillow case, and stuck the remaining coins in his pockets, his socks, and even into his prison-issue underwear.

He left his grandfather's house as quietly as he had entered.

When Chet climbed back into Johnston's car, he said, "Here it is: three hundred. Meet me back here tomorrow with the box after dark, I'll have the rest of the money for you. If I give you an extra ten bucks, will you drop me at the YMCA?"

"Sure thing, Nancy, you got a boyfriend there, too?"

Chet glowered at Johnston, said nothing.

"Aw, come on, I'm just breaking your balls. I don't mean anything by it. Doucette's twice your size and as mean as he is crazy. You're right to want his head, after what he did to you."

Chet nodded, his lips compressed in a stern line. "I think so."

After Johnston dropped him off within a block of the YMCA, Chet sat up all night in his room, chain-smoking his Asthmadors, and imagining all the brutal ways Johnston might liberate Doucette's head from his body. As the night wore on, his fantasies became more bloody and tortuous. He imagined that once he had Doucette's head in a box, maybe he'd be able to talk to it, maybe it might answer back . . .

Around dawn, Chet noticed that the walls of his small room were breathing—in, out, in, out—the same slow rhythm of Doucette's breathing when he was sleeping in his bunk below Chet in their cell.

"Wait, what?" Chet asked himself. *Something was wrong with me. Walls don't breathe. Doucette is not here with me in the YMCA. This is crazy stuff, real rubber room shit.* Chet tried to lie down on his bed, but moving made him nauseated. His head was pounding, his mouth dry. *Something is happening to me. I need a doctor.*

Slowly Chet made his way down to the front desk, stopping every few stairs so he didn't vomit. Weak and shaking, he held on to the reception desk with both hands, knuckles white.

The desk clerk stared at him. "Mister, you don't look right."

"You don't say," said Chet.

The young desk clerk, green enough to be immune to sarcasm, said, "Yeah, it's like your eyes are nothing but pupil. Did you smoke some reefer or something? We don't allow that at the YM . . ."

Chet vomited on the reception desk.

"Lemme help you over to those chairs, Mister, then I'm calling you a doctor."

Chet sat where the clerk put him while the room seemed to spin around him. *The walls of the lobby are breathing, too.*

After what seemed like an eternity, the doctor arrived. Chet couldn't exactly follow the doctor's conversation with the clerk, but there was some shouting, and Chet felt himself being lifted. *They are carrying me to a car?* Then nothing . . .

He came to in a crisp white hospital bed. Someone had sponged all the vomit off him, and dressed him in a thin cotton hospital gown. He had a rubber IV tube going into his left arm. His stomach hurt, his agonized throat felt raw, his head pounded. He was also jonesing for a cigarette.

He rang for a nurse. She entered the room, tall, middle-aged, green-eyed, used to be pretty. Her hair was in a tidy bun, her starched white nurse's cap perched on the top of her head.

He croaked, "Where's my smokes, my clothes, my money?" He struggled, but managed to sit up in his hospital bed.

The nurse scowled, the lines around her mouth deepening. "Your clothes are being laundered. Your money went into the safe. The cigarettes are the reason you are here, so I'm not giving them to you."

"What?"

"How many of those have you smoked in the last few days?"

"Maybe four packs?"

"Jesus, Mary, and Joseph, it's a wonder you are still alive."

"I don't understand"

"Those cigarettes, you aren't supposed to smoke that many."

"Why not? They're for my asthma!"

The nurse sighed. "Yes, for your asthma. Which means they are medicated." She nearly spat each syllable.

"Yeah, so?"

"So they contain belladonna leaves, not just tobacco—to say nothing of the tincture of opium—you've been poisoning yourself, you chump!" she said, her cheeks bright pink with irritation.

Chet shrugged. "Ok, what time is it? When can I leave?"

"You can't leave yet," she said, stern.

"Try and stop me,"

Her chest rose and fell as she took a deep calming breath. "Sir, you don't understand. We thought you had swallowed poison, so we pumped your stomach, gave you activated charcoal. It didn't help. We need to do something else. The poison wasn't in your stomach. We finally figured out you'd inhaled it. And you are not out of the woods yet."

"Meaning what?" Chet snapped.

"Meaning if you leave hospital right now, you will die. You might even die if you stay. Your only chance to survive is to stay here, get more treatment. We've sent for a poisoning specialist, and are just trying to keep you alive till he gets here. He has developed an antidote to belladonna poisoning, but now it's a race against time."

"You can say that again, sister." He glanced out the window at the glowering dusk. "What time is it?!" He was surprised he had the strength to shout.

The nurse sighed. "It's almost six pm. You got somewhere else to be rather than in hospital trying not to die?"

Chet swung his legs off the bed, and planted his feet on the floor. He was shaky but he could stand.

"As a matter of fact, I do. I gotta meet a guy and pay him for something, something important. And I don't need no lippy broad telling me what's what."

"Do you not understand that you will die if you leave?" Her hands were on her hips, her voice was loud, exasperated.

"Do you not understand that I don't give a rat's ass?" Chet shouted back.

The nurse turned on her heel and stalked out of the room. By the time he had yanked the IV from his arm, found a pair of hospital slippers, and put on a second hospital gown—backwards, so his ass was covered—she had returned with the gold coins and his last remaining tin of Asthmadors. Only three or four snipes left in the tin. He wanted one.

"I'll make you a deal, darlin'," Chet said, as he signed the form acknowledging that he was leaving against doctors' orders, "You call me a cab, and I won't light up another one of these darts until the cab pulls outta the parking lot."

"It's your funeral," she said, disgusted.

When Johnston pulled up in front of Chet's grandfather's house, the porchlight was on. He could see Chet, lying in a heap on the front porch next to a lumpy pillow case. Johnston picked up a newspaper-wrapped box from the floor of his '37 Ford, and set it—gingerly—beside Chet's body. The layers of newspaper, thick though they were, were damp and had started to seep red at the bottom corners. Johnston would need to clean the car tonight.

Satisfied with the heft of the pillowcase, Johnston walked back to his car, put it in gear, stomped on the gas pedal, and headed home to have dinner with his wife. It was pot-roast night.

Tight as a Nostril

Author's note: *The article referenced below concerned the Diva menstrual cup, an alternative to pads, tampons, and the like. Apparently Diva cups come in two sizes. One is designed for women who've never had vaginal child birth (VCB) and who are also under thirty years of age. The larger size Diva cup is intended for women who have experienced VCB or who are over thirty.*

The article was problematic. Given the overall tenor of Fusion *I was surprised to find something that might have been better placed at* Cosmopolitan. *So I wrote them a letter of complaint.*

Saturday, August 8, 2015
Letter of Complaint to *Fusion* Online Magazine

Hey there,

The article by Cleo Stiller on the Diva cup seems off-brand. I thought I understood your brand—maybe I don't, in which case it's my bad and I'll take my ball and go elsewhere on the Interwebz.

I found *Fusion* because I followed Jay Smooth here from You Tube. He's awesome. Tell him I say "hi", 'kay? I guess because he was involved I expected your writers to have a less problematic relationship with aging and with vaginas than the one evidenced in the article.

Do I really need to say that it's ok to get older? Do I really need to say that any kind of vagina is a nice vagina? Do I really need to say that concerns about the smallness and tightness of a woman's vagina suggest a stance wherein women and their vaginas exist primarily for the sexual pleasure of men who—apparently—can only get pleasing sexual friction from small, tight vaginas?

I bet no one over at *Fusion* actually thinks these things, at least not when they are stated so bluntly. I bet Stiller doesn't think these things. At least, I hope not. Eventually she will get older—if she is lucky—and her body, including her vagina, will change in ways she might not expect.

I sincerely hope that when that happens, she loves herself and stays grounded in her sexual and personal power. I hope she knows—with every cell—that her vagina and all her other body parts belong to her and exist for her pleasure and that when she shares her body with other people, everyone involved loves her and her body and they all have awesome toe-curling orgasms that leave them breathless and weeping . . . whether her vagina is wide, loose and sloppy, or tight as a nostril. Truly, I hope that for her, for everyone involved with *Fusion*, and for humans in general.

But I digress. Onward to my point: The article bugged me. It seemed ageist and sexist and body-shaming and kinda sex-phobic. Is that your brand? If it is, I'll go read something else. Maybe I'm in the wrong place. Please advise.

Best,

Chloe Cocking

Author's note: *I am hurt and surprised they did not write me back. I still think Jay Smooth is awesome, though.*

Hair of the Dog

The ship's mate punched Jonathan in the stomach. Jonathan doubled over, clutching his midsection and gasping for air. He did not have enough breath to scream. Then it was on: the four sailors beat him without mercy. The rough crowd loitering around the docks merely looked on with interest. Casual cruelty was their primary entertainment.

Though fourteen-year-old Jonathan was as tall as a man, he was thin and bony, something the miserly ship's rations over the past few months had done nothing to improve. He was no match for brawny adult men.

The sailor grabbed Jonathan by his blousy cotton shirt, dragging him upright, tearing the cloth. One of the other men landed a blow on Jonathan's jaw. He felt his lower lip split open, blood dribbling down his chin. The smallest of the sailors rabbit-punched Jonathan square on the nose while two others held Jonathan's arms. The cartilage cracked and blood gushed from Jonathan's nostrils. He could no longer smell dockside odours—salt water, decaying seaweed, rancid fish—now all he could smell was copper.

The ship's mate growled, "Let him go boys, I think one more punch will finish him." Jonathan felt himself wobble as he tried to stand on his own.

The ship's mate grabbed Jonathan's blood-splattered shirt front and swung a roundhouse punch at his head. The world teetered. Jonathan crumpled to the ground.

The men took turns kicking him as Jonathan curled in on himself. What seemed like hours passed as the men rained blows on him. They laughed while they did it. The on-looking crowd of rough men started calling out their bets. Which sailor will deliver the knock-out blow?

Finally, the four men paused. Jonathan, clenched into a ball on the wet boards of the dock, could hear them breathing heavily with the exertion. He could hear the crowd jeering. The ship's mate yanked Jonathan's right arm, stretching it out to its full extension. He brought his boot down on Jonathan's balled fist, stomping it again and again. The last thing Jonathan remembered was the ship's mate prying the worn leather pouch from his mangled fingers.

Jonathan moaned as his mind swam back to consciousness. *What is that unholy stench?* Every part of his body ached. One of his eyes was swollen shut, his nose was broken, his head throbbed, a couple of his teeth felt loose, and his lower lip was split like overripe fruit. Worst of all, his right hand looked like a bloody claw. The pain radiating from his twisted fingers stole Jonathan's breath and brought tears to his good eye. He blinked away the moisture. *Where am I? Where were the men who beat me? What is that smell?* He looked around.

"Where" was a narrow blind alley, wet stone walls on either side, capped with a grey March sky that threatened rain. The mouth of the alley opened on to a muddy street with no paving stones. The men were not in the alley with him. Jonathan said a quick prayer to the god he no longer believed in for that.

He staggered to his feet. He placed his uninjured left hand on one of the stone walls for support, and shuffled to the mouth of the blind alley. Every movement brought bile to his throat. He willed himself not to vomit the meagre contents of his stomach. He peered up and then down the muddy street. *No sailors in sight. No waterfront or docks, either.* Jonathan reckoned that the sailors must have dragged him here and simply left him for dead. *Welcome to the Virginia Colony.* Jonathan did not know whether to laugh at that thought, or sob in frustration. Instead he cleared his throat of phlegm, and spat a sticky clot of blood-tinged mucus on the ground.

He looked back to the blind end of the alley. The stench seemed to be coming from his only companion—the rotting corpse of a dead dog, lying on a bed of discarded cabbage leaves that carpeted the alley's slimy ground. Jonathan noticed both of the dog's eye sockets were empty and raw. *Eyes eaten by crows, I bet.* Jonathan shivered at the thought. He wrapped his arms around himself, cradling his ruined right hand.

He refused to dwell for long on what had happened. He couldn't afford to focus on the past—he had to keep moving forward. *I should have just given them the last of Father's money. They wouldn't have beat me and crushed my hand. Then at least I could have gotten some work, somewhere, somehow. Who will hire me now, with a ruined hand?* It started to rain. He could not imagine what he would do next.

* * *

Jonathan had—he thought—perfected the habit of ignoring the past while when he was on the ship carrying his family from England to the Virginia Colony.

At first, he thought only about the future because he didn't want to mope and pine for his old life. He could see it made Mother sad; when Mother was sad, his sisters would start bawling, and Father would shout at them and stalk off, red-faced.

During the journey from England, Jonathan allowed himself just a few reminiscences every week, doling them out to himself as treats. He would spend just moments imagining his old life: shopkeeper's only son, his mother teaching him how to keep the accounts. He had admired her beautiful penmanship, and had felt pride in the way she and his father spoke with customers—confident, at ease. Back in England he used to think *I want to be like Father when I grow up*.

That started to change when his father decided to sell everything and move the family to the Virginia Colony. The colony was giving every Englishman who arrived on their shore fifty acres of land. If he brought family with him, he'd receive another fifty acres for each additional person.

"That's two hundred and fifty acres," Father had crowed, bouncing Jonathan's younger sisters on his knee. Jonathan could tell from the tightness around his mother's mouth that she did not think it was a good idea. But she said nothing, at least not in front of him.

As the day of their departure grew closer, the lines around Mother's mouth were soon joined by ones between her brows. His little sisters did not want to go, either. They had cried when they learned of Father's plans. Jonathan did not.

"Chins up," he said to his little sisters, "Father will be a rich man, we will have land of our own, and you'll wear fine ribbons and ride on ponies like princesses."

The idea dried their tears and made their eyes sparkle. *Perhaps it will be true.*

Then came the sea voyage, the five of them sharing two hammocks below-deck. All the passengers—single men, mostly, and one other families—were housed in one small open room. His little sisters always managed to poke him with their elbows and knees while they slept in the hammock the three shared. His mother had begged nails and a hammer from the ship's mate, and tacked up one her petticoats to give the family some privacy from the other travelers. It turned out that was the last thing his father and mother could agree on.

Their disputes started before they had ever boarded the ship. One involved sour cabbage. When the family was preparing to leave England, Father had instructed Mother to put up a half-barrel of something called "sauerkraut" to bring on the journey. Father had explained that people on ships often got a sickness called scurvy. Eating some of this sauerkraut every day prevented it, Father had said. There were other ways, but they were much more costly. Jonathan had hoped there was something magical about this sauerkraut, but it turns out it was just pickled cabbage.

Almost everything about the journey was similarly disappointing. Still, Jonathan had tried to keep his spirits up, daydreaming about all that he would do on the acres of land Father would get one in the colonies.

It distracted him from his parents fighting in urgent whispers when they thought the children were asleep.

"Charles, surely you cannot be serious!" his mother had whispered one night.

"No, Sarah, I am serious, I am trying to protect this family. We will have none left for our own health—"

"They are just children, Charles! If it were our children, wouldn't you want someone to help?"

"I would, but they are not. Their care rests with their own family, not with mine."

"Charles, please . . ."

"No. Enough of this, woman, sleep now! We have trouble enough of our own."

But Mother did not sleep that night. As soon as Father drifted off, snoring gently, Jonathan saw her slip out of the hammock, and wrap herself in a woolen blanket. Pretending to be asleep, he saw her climb the ladder to the hatch that led to the deck, so she could pace and think without waking anyone.

When she returned, hours later, it was nearing dawn, and light enough that he could see her eyes were red, her face puffy, and that she was soaked to the skin. She dried herself as best she could on the petticoat-curtain. She climbed back into the hammock slowly, trying not to disturb Father.

Four days later she was dead. Jonathan did not know whether Mother had caught whatever ailed the children she had wanted to give sauerkraut to, or whether she sickened and died from being out all night in the cold rain. He would hear her wet weak coughing in his dreams for the rest of his life.

Mother wasn't the only one who died. Both his sisters passed only a few days after Mother had. Like Mother, they were buried at sea, the Captain saying a few words.

Within the week, the captain was performing this ritual every day. Many hammocks swung empty, no people to fill them. Jonathan kept eating sauerkraut almost as a sacrament. He thought of his Mother with every bite. He tried not to think of Father.

After the girls died, Father started to pay coins to some of the seamen for a share in their rum and a few hands of cards. Jonathan swung in his hammock, alone, rocked gently by the ocean. He forced himself to stop thinking of the past. He did not want to think of Mother and the girls, eaten by fish at the bottom of the ocean. He did not want to be a man like his father, not anymore.

Two days before land was sighted, Jonathan's father died from choking on his own vomit. Too drunk to climb into a hammock, Father had passed out on his back on the floor and choked to death while the remaining passengers—Jonathan included—slept deeply. Jonathan wondered if he had been woken up by Father's strangling and sputtering, would he have helped him? Or would he have merely turned over in his hammock and stared at the splintery wall? Jonathan did not know. He helped the ship's mate carry Father's body up to the deck. He helped heave it over the side after the Captain, weaving on his feet and reeking of rum, said a slurred prayer.

The seamen teased Jonathan—did Jonathan want to take his father's place at cards and enjoy some rum as well? After all, there were still coins left in Father's leather pouch. Jonathan declined, and kept to himself. The seamen frightened him. He tied the pouch around his waist underneath his clothes to keep it safe. He would need something for lodging and food in the Colonies until he could get a job.

* * *

Seven months after the sailors had left him for dead in an alley in Norfolk, Jonathan had sussed out a survival routine.

Just before dawn every day, he knocked on bakery doors, begging any scraps of dough or burned buns they couldn't sell.

After the bakeries, he sidled around the central market in Norfolk; Jonathan knew all the right stalls to steal from. There were two times that were best to steal: when the market was very busy, the vendors preoccupied with customers, and the times the market was almost empty. When the market was slow, the women and men who minded the stalls would get bored, and leave their stations unattended so they could gossip and flirt. Their wares were easy pickings for Jonathan. He had learned to be as quick with his left hand as he had been with his now-ruined right.

After pinching what he could from the market, Jonathan would usually walk some ways out from town and nap under a tree or bush, hidden from any passersby. He did not like to sleep at night or in town. Men had approached him with a gleam in their eyes too often. He knew what that gleam meant from bitter recent experience. He took care to sleep during the day, and then only when well-hidden from sight.

After the sun went down, he usually walked back into town so he could circulate in or near the crowded pub, picking pockets as the opportunity arose. The first time he tried it, the pub owner caught him and thrashed him, but Jonathan came back the next day with a proposal: if the owner looked the other way while Jonathan picked pockets, Jonathan would pay him half the night's takings for the privilege. The owner, a beefy red-faced man with watery seeping eyes, agreed.

The first frosty night in late October, Jonathan was circulating in the pub, and had almost removed a few coins from a large man's pocket when the man's scrawny companion grasped Jonathan's wrist.

"Well me boy, there's no need for that," he hissed, his breath foul.

Jonathan noticed two of the small man's front teeth were blackened nubs. He tried to pull his wrist away from the small man, but his grip was like iron.

"Max," said the small man, addressing his burly companion, "what should we do with a lad whot's got his hand in your pocket?"

The larger man turned around, regarded Jonathan. "Looks too skinny to eat," he said at last.

"I was thinking the same meself, actually. Perhaps we should sit with this lad, give 'im the benefit of our experience?"

"I think the way you think, Bill, you can always spot a young man who needs our counsel. What say you, boy? Will you sit and eat soup with us?"

Jonathan was dumbfounded. Surely these men meant to beat him for trying to steal from them. He looked around the room for the pub owner. *Nowhere to be seen, of course.*

"Looks like he's afraid we'll thrash him," said Bill.

"He should be." Max smiled under his beard, eyes cold like shards of flint.

"Now, now, let's not be like that, Max, remember your Christian charity and all that." Bill winked at Max.

"Fine, fine," said Max, "Listen up, lad, here is how this works. Eat a bowl or two of soup with us and we *won't* thrash you. And we'll have a few drinks as well, you like rum, don't you boy?"

Jonathan was confused. "Why would you help me?"

Bill feigned mock horror. "Look at this Max, will you? Still but a lad and already he thinks the world is a hard place. Give us a chance to do our Christian duty, will you?"

Max smiled. "We really won't take 'no' for an answer, lad."

* * *

Jonathan woke up on a pile of greasy ropes in the store room of a ship. His head throbbed from last night's rum, he had a painful kink in his neck, and his ragged clothes were covered with his own dried vomit. He was bound hand and foot. He blinked at his surroundings, trying to gather his wits. *What the hell happened last night?*

The rough-hewn door flew open, and a stout, middle-aged woman entered. She was taller than most men, dressed in men's canvas breeches, a stained white tunic, and knee-high boots. She wore her salt-and-pepper hair in a single long plait down her back. An enormous macaw—with brilliant red, blue, and yellow feathers—perched on her left shoulder.

The woman scratched the feathers on the bird's neck with her hardened fingers. "Welcome to *Hair of the Dog*. You're in my service now."

"In my service!" shrieked the parrot.

Jonathan winced, tried to sit up straight, failed. He cleared his sore throat. "Kidnapped, am I?"

The woman smiled, but only with her mouth, not with her eyes. "Not kidnapped, boy, crimped."

The parrot bounced up and down on her shoulder. "Crimped and pimped! Crimped and pimped and slimped and crimped! Ha-ha-ha-ah!"

The woman removed a shelled cashew from a pocket in her breeches, and fed it to the bird. "Shush, you, be quiet now."

Stepping closer to Jonathan, she drew a knife from her belt. He could feel his eyes grow round as he gasped. *This is it—she's going to murder me!* She started to saw at the rope that bound his ankles.

"I'm your captain. Just call me 'Cap'n.' The bundle of gaudy feathers on my shoulder is known as 'Husband'. Mind your fingers near him, he likes to bite little boys."

"I'm Jonathan."

"So you told my crimpers last night as they kept filling your cup." She continued to saw at the ropes.

"Crimpers?"

Husband whistled, and Captain fed him another cashew. "Crimpers is what you call my agents on shore; they find me new recruits when we need them."

Jonathan sniffed. That made the pounding in his head worse. He was so thirsty. "So you send them out to find a fool, get him drunk, and bring him back here?"

Captain freed his ankles and started to saw on the ropes that bound Jonathan's wrists. "I hope you're not a fool, you won't last long with me if you are. But you have the look of an educated lad about you, hopefully you'll join my crew peaceably and without complaint." She tucked her knife back into the sheath strapped to her thigh.

Jonathan rubbed his chaffed wrists. To his horror, his eyes filled with tears. *No no be brave be brave.* Tears spilled down his cheeks and he half-coughed, half-sobbed.

"Boo hoo hoo booo hoo hooooo," said Husband as he bounced off the Captain's shoulder. With stiff legs, Husband hopped to a pile of malodorous rags near Jonathan and perched there, tilting his head, inspecting Jonathan with his shiny onyx-bead eyes.

"Oh, Husband, do be quiet. I am training our new recruit."

Captain tossed the parrot another cashew from her pocket, stepped back from Jonathan, and leaned against a barrel. She patted the pockets of her trousers, drew out a corncob pipe, and started tamping down the contents of the pipe bowl with her thumb. She struck a match on the sole of her boot, puffed on the pipe stem, and looked him in the eye. "So tell me, boy, how old are you?"

"Fourteen last February."

"Are you an educated lad?" Her round face was wreathed in smoke.

"I can read, and write, and figure sums." He squared his shoulders.

"Even with that?" she asked, nodding at Jonathan's twisted right hand.

"I can learn to write with the other if I have to. I can do anything, if I have to," Jonathan said.

Captain smoked and thought for a few moments, while Husband bobbed stiff-legged all over the store room, poking his head into sacks, and sampling what was inside.

"Good thing you have brains. I've got brawn to spare on my crew, but brains are in short supply."

"What if I don't want to work on *Hair of the Dog*?"

Captain's smiled, hard and insincere. She held a hand out to Husband, who jumped on and allowed himself to be placed on Captain's shoulder again.

"Come topside with me, boy."

Jonathan followed the woman and the parrot up the ladder and through a hatch she opened. Every step he took, every rung he climbed made his head pound. As he clamboured out onto the deck, he could feel the sun hammering his hatless head. The bright sunlight made him feel like each of his temples was pierced with a nail.

A sailor a few feet from the hatch was applying hot tar to a section of the deck. Other people shouted at each from far above; they had climbed the rigging, and were making adjustments and repairs. The smell of the hot pitch and the salt ocean mixing in his nostrils made his stomach lurch. Mouth suddenly full of saliva, he clenched his eyes shut and willed himself not vomit.

Captain stroked the parrot's feathered head with one hand, waiting for Jonathon to adjust. When he finally opened his eyes, she pointed to a smear on the horizon.

"See that?"

"Yes."

"That's where we come from. You're welcome to swim back."

"Swim-swim!" demanded Husband.

Jonathan sighed, and squared his shoulders again.

"You can start by looking over the sums in the trading books. I think the bloody quartermaster is cheating me, but I'm not certain."

Jonathan thought for a moment. "Because you can't read?"

Husband started squawking and flapping, and Captain's face was unreadable. Jonathan saw her eyes harden, confirming his guess.

"I need a smart boy, an educated boy." Captain looked at Jonathan, eyebrows raised. "A boy who keeps himself to himself, discreetly."

"Understood. Ma'am."

"Just call me 'Cap'n' like all the rest."

Husband flapped his wings. "Cap'n Cap'n—who's a pretty boy?" Captain fed Husband another cashew.

"Cap'n?" Jonathan asked.

"Yes?"

"Can I have some water before I start with them books? My head wicked throbs."

Cap'n reached into her back pocket and pulled out a dented metal flask. "Hair of the dog that bit ya will be better for your particular ailment, lad."

She held the flask out, and Jonathan grabbed it. He took a heroic swig. Looking out to the horizon, he knew that trying to swim was pointless. Even if he didn't drown on the way back to shore, there was nothing to swim back to. A pirate he would be.

Janice's Secret

Seattle, 2003

She's got to keep it a secret. She'll be kidnapped otherwise.

Janice stared at the AIM pop-up on her computer screen. She swirled the half-melted ice in the bottom of her glass.

She'd been staring at the pop-up since it appeared ten minutes ago. Everything and nothing was running through Janice's mind, but she felt cool, composed. This blessed dispassion was provided by the Johnnie Walker she'd been sipping. It was the only thing that could calm her.

Six months ago, Mike left her and their thirteen-year-old daughter, Suzanne. Janice had been livid at his betrayal. When Mike grabbed his suitcase and walked down the front path for the last time, something about the jaunty set of his shoulders enraged her. *He looks chipper now that he's left this behind.* She had fantasied running up behind him, jumping on his disappearing back, and pounding on him with her fists. Instead Janice had screamed, "It was supposed to be for better or worse, in sickness or in health, asshole!" Mike did not turn around, not even to give her the finger. Those unburdened shoulders didn't even twitch.

Mike leaving left Janice sad, overwhelmed, and

trying hard to put a cheerful face on it for Suzanne's sake. All of it made Janice so anxious she could not sleep. Something about being the only adult in the home, solely responsible for Suzanne, made her tense. Her nights were fretful; trying different bed postures, flipping her pillow over to enjoy the cool side against her cheek, adjusting and re-adjusting the blinds in her bedroom. So Janice had started to enjoy a bedtime cocktail; then she could relax enough to go to sleep.

About three weeks ago, one bedtime cocktail turned into three or four. As soon as Suzanne kissed her mother's cheek and turned in for the night, Janice started thinking about drinking. Janice felt that there was a switch inside her that toggled from "mother" to "person". Janice used the "mother" setting all day long: going to work at her job to earn money to support the two of them, taking Suzanne to this psychiatrist or that mental health clinic, cooking supper, supervising Suzanne's homework, trying to remain positive despite what they were going through. After Suzanne went to bed, the switch toggled to the "person" setting, and the whiskey started to flow.

She was just pouring herself another drink when her computer made the "ba-bink" sound that meant another message had arrived.

Walking over to her computer, she saw that PapaBear (real name unknown) had messaged her again.

Mama1961, still there?

Yes, still here, Janice typed.

Is what I'm saying making any sense? asked PapaBear.

Yes . . . but . . .

. . . But what? U R wondering?

Janice sighed, put her heavy-bottomed glass down on the desk, and typed with both hands. *I am wondering how to make this right for my daughter, how to help her have a normal life.*

The status bar on the instant messaging pop-up said "PapaBear is typing a message . . .". Janice sipped whiskey and watched the dots in the ellipse shiver as somewhere in the world PapaBear typed.

You are not going to like what I have to say on this. I'm sorry about that. But it needs to be said—her options for normal evaporated the day she was diagnosed with necromancy.

Janice felt her eyes prickle with tears. She typed: *But that's so goddamn unfair!*

Is it fair that your husband left when the going got tough? Is it fair that she's being bullied in school? Is it fair that it took the mental health system six months to differentiate speaking with the dead from psychosis or early onset schizophrenia? NONE of this is fucking fair, to anyone.

Janice sighed, and chewed an ice cube as she stared at the screen. "PapaBear is typing . . ."

Mama1961, I feel you, I really do. But you've got to woman-up. YOU are the only one who can keep her safe, you are all she's got.

Janice started to cry in earnest now. She typed: *Fuck my ex for bailing on her, for bailing on both of us. Fuck the mental health system that took so long to figure out what the hell was wrong with my kid. Fuck it all.*

Agreed. Your ex is a douche and a goddamn coward. I'm one of the only dads on this board, and it makes me ashamed of my entire gender that so many men lam it when the going gets tough. That said, you can do this. You can protect her. It won't be easy, but you can do it.

Janice had tears running down her face. She was glad that Suzanne was in bed asleep. The only light in the living room came from the computer screen. She didn't want her girl to see her cry.

Mama1961, you ok?

Processing it right now. And crying. Plus I'm a bit drunk, to tell the truth.

Atta girl. Do what you gotta do, I'm not gonna judge.

Janice cried harder and typed *thnx*

What's the hardest part of this for you, the worst of the worst?

Hmm . . . aside from the sheer fact that she's gonna have to live with this for the rest of her life? Probably the tinfoil hat parts.

Lolz. Like all the stuff that seems far-fetched?

Yeah. At risk for kidnapping? Secret government labs? Unethical experiments on supernaturals?

I know! I remember feeling that way when we learned about my son's telekinesis. It took me a while to accept it. It's like processing a death kinda, you know the stages of grief around death and dying?

Yeah, like on that Simpsons *episode where Dr. Hibbert tells Homer he has twenty-four hours to live, and Homer goes through denial, anger, bargaining, depression, and then acceptance, all in about five seconds?*

Lolz. That's the one!

AIM said "PapaBear is typing a message . . ." Ba-bink!

Not gonna be five seconds, though.

Fuck.

Yup.

Janice stood up from her chair and stretched. "Getting late, I should sign off soon. I might even be able to sleep tonight," she thought.

She looked back at the computer screen. The AIM window displayed the jumping dots: "PapaBear is typing a message".

Read this, ok? Then we'll talk more tomorrow

AIM asked, "Papa Bear would like to send you a file. Do you accept?"

Janice clicked on the accept button.

AIM announced "Josie's_Story.txt is downloading".

Janice typed: *What is it?*

AngelKissed, the lady who started the bulletin board for parents of supernaturals, wrote it. It's what happened to her daughter. Or what she knows of it, anyway.

Why doesn't she know all of it?

Just read it, you'll see. It's a hard and scary read. But you are stronger than you think, and you need to know what's out there, potentially.

Janice eyes got wet again. *Ok* she typed.

I'll be in the BBS chat room and on AIM anytime after 5PM Greenwich time tomorrow, talk more then?

Yes. G'nite PapaBear. Thanks for all that you do.

De nada, Mama1961. We gotta stick together.

Janice opened her download folder, right clicked on the document and selected 'print'. "Looks like I'm not gonna sleep tonight after all," she thought.

The Deli Cat

The deli on Royal Avenue had been owned by the same family of gangsters for over seventy years. The combination of community longevity and ongoing criminality meant that Royal's Deli could break many of the rules.

Back in the 1980's, before Sunday shopping was legal, they were open anyway. The building had never been renovated or brought up to fire code—it managed to survive as a business without sprinklers or even a smoke alarm. But perhaps the most flagrant violation of municipal rules was relatively new: Hortensia.

Hortensia was an eighteen-pound tortoiseshell cat who had lived in the deli full-time for the past five years. This went against every health code imaginable.

Foul-tempered and mercurial, she presided over the premises with a haughty air. On cold rainy days, she slept in a sweatshirt nest on top of the industrial stainless steel fridge behind the deli counter. On sunny days, she lay claim to the tiled surface of the bistro table set in the middle of the front window. She wandered the counters at will, removing tidbits of meat and cheese from orders as they were being prepared. Sometimes, if a customer left a wrapped packet of deli meat unattended too long, Hortensia would drag it away to her hiding place under the back counter. She guarded her prey jealously. She growled savagely if approached. Eventually, with pointed tooth and razor claw, she would disembowel her paper prize so she could feast on the mortadella or salami inside.

Customers not in the know would sometimes complain about Hortensia. Once. Deli staff and even regulars would chastise the complainant. "Take your business over to Save-On-Foods if you don't like how we do it here," one of the staff would say.

Deli regulars were even blunter about it, usually with a terse, "Shut the fuck up about it, it's not your business."

Hortensia was in great favour at the deli because she was beloved by the current crime kingpin of New Westminster, Mike Finitis. Mike was a large man. He stood well over six feet tall, and weighed at least two hundred and eighty pounds. His left eyebrow was bisected by a scar he got in a knife fight in his teens. His cheeks were pitted with old acne scars. His dark hair was full and glossy even though it was threaded with silver. He dressed flamboyantly, in well-cut suits, bespoke shirts, and carved gold rings. They glinted in the sun when he sipped espresso from a tiny demitasse cup at the bistro table. Hortensia was his constant companion. When Mike held court at the deli, she sprawled over the surface of the table, basking in the sunlight and Mike's adoration.

Even Mike was not safe from Hortensia's bad temper. Sometimes, for no reason anyone could determine, Hortensia would leap from the bistro table to Mike's belly, scratch at him with her claws, then bound away making an ear-shattering caterwaul. Mike accepted this with equanimity, even when her claws snagged the lapels of his fine suit.

Mike's love for Hortensia was so great, it played into his business dealings. Once a rival gangster sat down with Mike at the bistro table. As usual, Hortensia was sprawled over the table surface, meticulously cleaning an outstretched claw on her right front paw.

The rival looked at her with disgust, made a scornful sound, and pushed Hortensia to the floor. Surprised but uninjured, she stalked away. Haughty, her tail a tri-coloured arrow pointing at the ceiling.

Mike said nothing, but the emotional tone of the room changed. People who knew Mike well expected the worst. No one knows what happened, but after a week had passed, the rival disappeared. Rumour had it that he was at the bottom of the Fraser river.

Not only did Hortensia have the run of the deli itself, she was allowed to come and go as she pleased via a custom cat door installed in the back entrance. Her access to the outdoors was a problem, as she had never been spayed. "It's unnatural," Mike said, when someone suggested it. It was not mentioned again. As a result, Hortensia had at least one litter of kittens every year.

Whatever the circumstances of Hortensia's genetics, or those of the toms she mated with, every litter so far had been comprised entirely of tortoiseshell kittens—all female, as virtually all tortoiseshell cats are.

Not only did all the kitties look like Hortensia, most had all inherited her complex and troubling personality. No one had ever seen Hortensia near other cats, so no one knew for sure which of the unaltered toms in the neighbourhood had fathered the litters. Sometimes deli staff joked that Hortensia's pregnancies were parthenogenic.

The deli staff were charged with giving away the little kitties after Hortensia weaned them. They tried many different promotions: "Free kitten with every 500 grams of grana padano purchased" and "Get twelve spicy sausages for the price of six, plus a free kitten".

The deli's customers from the straight world were much more interested in cheese and sausage than kittens. Some of the customers connected to crime would take a free kitty simply to curry favour with Mike. However, there were always more kitties, since Hortensia's fecundity was as prodigious as her belly.

Eventually Mike stepped in with a solution: whenever Mike sent his bag men to collect the weekly vig owed by gamblers, they were given a kitten. If, over the next few weeks, the kitten appeared well-cared for and happy in her new home, a few percentage points were shaved off the vig.

In the five years since Hortensia had lived in the deli, she had produced a few dozen kittens. At this point, the pet population in Queensborough neighbourhoods adjacent to the casino were populated entirely by large surly tortoiseshell cats.

Like all cats who have uncontrolled access to the outdoors, Hortensia was at risk of being run over by cars. About once a year, Mike's wife reminded him of this fact. She begged him to remove the cat door from the deli. Mike felt that people driving down Royal Avenue should show him (and Hortensia) the proper respect. He had ruled for decades and was used to deference. He saw no reason for respect to stop just because someone was behind the wheel of a car.

Mike's wife knew there was no point in mentioning that, these days, Royal Avenue was a thru-highway and most people taking that route had no idea who Mike was, that his reputation was well-deserved, nor that Mike was devoted to his cat. Privately, Mike's wife thought it was only a matter of time before something happened to poor Hortensia.

Her prediction came to life one day in March. Hortensia had been basking in a spot of early spring sunshine. Terry, the mechanic who worked at the import car repair shop next door to the deli, had noticed her as he headed to the deli for a sandwich. Instead of entering the deli to stand in line, he paused for a moment to scratch Hortensia behind the ears.

Hortensia was not having it. She hissed at Terry, and darted across Royal Avenue. Mercifully, the traffic light closest to the deli was red.

Terry was alarmed. Lunch time traffic was heavy. He liked cats, and wanted no harm to come to her. He also liked his legs unbroken.

Just as the streetlights turned green, Hortensia lay down on the yellow line in the middle of the road. Terry bounded after the cat, waving his arms and shouting. All four lanes of traffic stopped, and Terry scooped her up in his arms.

Hortensia struggled with Terry, biting and clawing him as he trotted back toward the north side of Royal Avenue. Terry was so distracted by the cat's attack, he did not see the cyclist barreling down the hill. What the cyclist saw was anyone's guess; whatever it was, it certainly wasn't Terry struggling with 18 pounds of irascible feline.

When the cyclist hit Terry, police estimated the bicycle was travelling at least forty kilometres per hour. Terry, arms full of struggling cat, could not brace himself. He made a one-point landing on his left knee, shattering his patella. Hortensia bit Terry as she lept from his arms to the safety of the sidewalk. She took a loonie-sized chunk of his hand with her. The cyclist flew off his bicycle and skidded ten feet on the pavement, using his face for brakes.

Mike saw it all from the deli window. He came outside, scooped his cat up under one arm, and dialed 9-1-1 on his cell phone with his free hand. While he spoke on the phone with the 9-1-1 operator, Mike kicked the prostrate cyclist in the kidneys a few times.

Hortensia, tucked like a furry football under Mike's left arm, finished chewing the morsel of flesh she had gouged from Terry's hand. Eyeing Terry coolly as he lay on the concrete, she started to clean her paws.

The next day a fat envelope of cash was dropped anonymously into the car repair shop's mail slot. Mike had the cat door removed. Mike's wife pretended that it had been Mike's idea all along. Hortensia stayed inside the deli, until Mike trained her to accept a harness and leash. He walked her once a day. From then on, she was the terror of the dog park on Carnarvon Street.

My Books Have Disappeared

EMAIL TO: a major e-book retailer
February 10, 2012

Hi there,

I was tidying up my "I'm reading" list on the <redacted> site. I deleted 100 or so books, assuming that they would remain in "my purchases" list. This has always been the case when I have cleaned up the "I'm reading" list in the past.

This time, they did not remain. "My purchases" list reflects the same eight volumes I kept in my "I'm reading" list. In other words, over one hundred books are missing and I don't know how to get them back.

Did I do something wrong, or is there a hiccup on your end? I have logged out and then in again several times, on multiple devices, including devices that I have never used before now.

Please help! One hundred lost e-books is over $1,000 dollars' worth of purchases! With empty virtual shelves, regards from the very upset,

Chloe Cocking

EMAIL FROM: <redacted> Customer Care
February 10, 2012

Thank you for contacting <redacted> Customer Care. Please accept this notification as confirmation we have received your email. We will be in touch via email within twenty-four hours to help resolve the problem.

Author's Note: *Five days passed without word.*

> EMAIL FROM: <redacted> Customer Care
> February 15, 2012

Recently you requested personal assistance from our on-line support center. Below is a summary of your request and our response. If this issue is not resolved to your satisfaction, you may reopen it within the next 10 days. Thank you for allowing us to be of service to you.

Good Day Ms. Cocking,

I am sorry that you are missing your book that you were cleaning off your account. I have checked your Purchase History and I do in fact see the book still there. Could I get you to sign out of your account on the website and then re-log in to the account to see if the books will appear back in your Purchases. Books that you purchase through <redacted> will never disappear and we are able to load them back on your account.

While we have marked this ticket as solved, rest assured this ticket will remain eligible for re-opening should the suggested solution prove unsuccessful. To reopen your ticket, simply respond to the ticket notifying us of the current status and a member of our

Customer Care team will review your response and action accordingly.

If we do not hear from you within the next 10 days, we will assume the suggested solution was successful and we will retire your ticket.

Sincerely,
The <redacted> Customer Care Team

> EMAIL TO: *a major e-book retailer*
> *February 15, 2012*

Hi there,

Unfortunately my issue is not resolved. I would like the issue re-opened. Also, can this issue be escalated to a supervisor or second tier tech?

Best,
Chloe Cocking

EMAIL FROM: <redacted> Customer Care
February 18, 2012

Recently you requested personal assistance from our on-line support center. Below is a summary of your request and our response. If this issue is not resolved to your satisfaction, you may reopen it within the next 10 days. Thank you for allowing us to be of service to you.

Good Day Ms. Cocking,

Please try logging out and then back in again. You might also want to shut your computer down or try to access our site with another device. Books that you purchase through <redacted> will never disappear and we are able to load them back on your account.

While we have marked this ticket as resolved, rest assured this ticket will remain eligible for re-opening should the suggested solution prove unsuccessful. To reopen your ticket, simply respond to the ticket notifying us of the current status and a member of our Customer Care team will review your response and action accordingly.

If we do not hear from you within the next 10 days, we will assume the suggested solution was successful and we will retire your ticket.

Sincerely,
The <redacted> Customer Care Team

> EMAIL TO: a major e-book retailer
> February 18, 2012

Hey there humans,

Unfortunately my issue is not resolved. I would like the issue re-opened. Also, can this issue be escalated to a supervisor or second tier tech? The exchange we have had so far has not inspired confidence. Not feeling warm nor fuzzy. In fact, if the response I received wasn't mere customer service bafflegab, I'd be starting to think you guys don't like me.

HERE IS THE PROBLEM:

Over ONE HUNDRED BOOKS I have purchased from <redacted> since May 2010 are missing from my "My purchases" list. Right now there are eight in there, there should be in excess of one hundred. I want you guys to fix this.

(How's that for a clear, direct succinct statement of the problem and the desired solution? I am so awesome. My anger management coach would be so proud of me.)

To further this conversation and prevent any more unintentionally hilarious yet simultaneously insulting emails from you kind folks, let me stipulate the following so we don't re-tread old ground:

1. I'm not complaining there are NO books in the list. There are, in fact, eight. If you guys log in, you'll look and see that there are eight. That's what the first tech did. In fact, the tech was so satisfied that was all that was necessary, that was all that was done. Well, that and a boilerplate email that expresses how happy <redacted> is to be able to serve me, etc. It is fantastic to get email like that during a process that demonstrates the exact opposite.

If I were to suggest your 'customer care' processes are rather Orwellian, would it hurt your feelings or offend your dignity? I hope so.

Know also that for every boilerplate email you lob at me, I have yet another excellent story to tell people in bars. I've been drinking for free for days now because of you guys. At this rate, I won't have a chance to sober up until spring. Do you really want my incipient alcoholism to be on your collective heads, Customer Care Team?

Be that as it may, I shall press onward to my point:

While it is grand that we now all agree there are eight books in "My purchases," sadly it doesn't fix my problem.

This issue is that there should be over one hundred books in "My Purchases" list but there are not.

I am really hoping that now that I've stated the issue three times so far in this email that my point has actually landed. My first email was not absorbed properly, so I figure by using humour, sarcasm, and boring repetition, I may reach a person who can actually help me with this.

(*sigh* a girl can dream, can't she?)

2. As I mentioned in my first email, I have done the basics like logging in and out of <redacted>. I have done this several times, on various devices, re-starting the devices before each attempt.

I have logged in here and there and everywhere: on my laptop, on my netbook, on my tablet, and my smart phone, on my work computer, and on my colleague's work computer. I have logged in and out and up and down. I have logged in with a fox, on a box, in a train, down the drain, with green eggs and ham, with one fish, two fish, red fish, blue fish.

Then I logged in one more time, just to be sure.

The result? **I am satisfied this is not a data-caching issue, as your response seems to suggest.**

The email you folks sent me states "Books that you purchase through <redacted> will never disappear and we are able to load them back on your account".

It'd be peachy keen if someone there could do that for me.

Thanks

Chloe Cocking
- Disgruntled
- Curiously without a hundred or so books
- Feeling cranky about techs who either don't read or don't understand the issue at hand

Author's Note: *Six days passed without word from so-called Customer Care.*

EMAIL FROM: <Redacted> Customer Care

February 24 2012

While we have marked this ticket as solved, rest assured this ticket will remain eligible for re-opening should the suggested solution prove unsuccessful. To reopen your ticket, simply respond to the ticket notifying us of the current status and a member of our Customer Care team will review your response and action accordingly.

If we do not hear from you within the next 10 days, we will assume the suggested solution was successful and we will retire your ticket.

Sincerely,
The <redacted> Customer Care Team

>   EMAIL TO: a major e-book retailer
>   February 24 2012

Yo, Dopes!

So that's how you're going to do me, after all this? Send me more boilerplate?

Again, I request that issue be escalated to a supervisor or second-tier tech. The issue is not resolved. Purchases I have made on your site are not reflected in "my purchases". Please fix this.

Love and kisses,

Chloe Cocking

- Not yet re-gruntled
- Still missing 100+ books
- Full of existential despair because of this customer service experience

EMAIL FROM: <Redacted> Customer Care
February 25 2012

While we have marked this ticket as solved, rest assured this ticket will remain eligible for re-opening should the suggested solution prove unsuccessful. To reopen your ticket, simply respond to the ticket notifying us of the current status and a member of our Customer Care team will review your response and action accordingly.

If we do not hear from you within the next 10 days, we will assume the suggested solution was successful and we will retire your ticket.

Sincerely,
The <redacted> Customer Care Team

EMAIL TO: a major e-book retailer
February 25 2012

Hey, You Graceless Bags of Mostly Water—

Attached please find electronic receipts for one hundred and three e-book purchases I have made at <redacted>. You'll notice that none of these titles currently appear in "my purchases".

Fix it. Do it now.

You don't want to mess with me further as I have:

- a lot of time on my hands
- no sense of proportion
- Level 38 ninja skills when it comes to Google-stalking

With that warning in mind, please also consider that **I am officially at the end of my motherfucking tether.**

What does that mean for you?

Long after you've forgotten these exchanges, long after you've left the so-called Customer Care Team at <redacted>, I will find you and all the people you love.

I will slip rotten prawns into your curtain rods.

That's right: in the dead of a humid summer night, I will sneak in to all of your homes, unscrew your finials, and stuff raw shellfish into the hollow rods. The smell will increase over days and weeks. It will be unbearable. You will not be able to find the origin.

Go ahead, send your curtains out to be dry-cleaned, that can't save you now.

You know what will?

Restoring the one hundred and three books I have purchased from <redacted> to "My Purchases" in my account (receipts attached).

Have a blessed day,

Chloe Cocking,
Mistress of Seafood-based Revenge Schemes

Author's Note: *Twenty minutes after I pressed "send" on the email above, the books were magically restored to my account. They did not send me an email advising me on the status of my trouble ticket. To date, the RCMP have yet to contact me about my threats. My fantasies of seafood-based revenge remain just that, fantasies . . . so far.*

Thirty-Five Arrested After Riot in Vegan Strip Club

Kalee stifled a sigh as she rubbed John's face in her sweaty cleavage. She tossed her long black hair over one shoulder in a practiced gesture. Wednesday nights were always a very slow night for lap dances. Club Vee was particularly empty tonight. Privately, Kalee blamed all the late night Christmas shopping extravaganzas. Almost all of her mid-week regulars were standing in line to buy IPhones or Xboxes or some such shit. There were only four shopping days left until Christmas. The only regular who had come in tonight was John. Of course, he was the one Kalee liked the least.

It wasn't that John was intimidating or threatening. He was just so awkward. He spilled his drink at least once every evening. He never realized when he had spinach in his teeth. His personal hygiene left something to be desired, and worst of all, he thought he was witty and charming.

Tonight was no different than any Wednesday since Club Vee had launched. He appeared about fifteen minutes after the club opened, ate three plates of food from the vegan buffet, and stared expectantly at the stage until the first dancer came on. When Kalee started to circulate among the customers, offering lap dances, he had greeted her as he always did. "Heeeey, bouncy Miss Kalee! Good to see you, sexy mama. Tell me, is the vee in Club Vee for 'vegan' or for 'va-jay-

jay'?" Then he smiled with satisfaction, as though this was the cleverest thing imaginable.

Kalee's own sense of humour trended more to the absurd—dysfunctional cheese shops, ex-parrots—but she pasted a grin on her face and giggled anyway. All part of being professional on the job, after all.

Kalee took a step back from John's lap and turned around. She bent her widespread legs and placed her hands on her hips. She started to twerk just a couple of inches over John's lap. Snapping her pelvis to the tempo of the hip-hop blasting from the club's sound system, Kalee reflected that it wasn't just John's sexism or his tedious repetition that annoyed her. She was aware there were boring and cheesy people in every workplace. No, what bothered Kalee was how disrespectful John could be to the concept of veganism itself. *Why does he bother to come to a vegan club if he hates veganism so much? It doesn't make any sense. He could go to Klassi Ladieeezzz over on Templeton just as easily.*

Kalee turned around, once again stuffing John's face into her cleavage. *And that's the other thing—for a guy who claims he hates "rabbit food", he can sure pack away the saag soy paneer, all while complaining we don't serve hot wings. Who does that? Can't the vegans of Portland have one meat-free sexually-themed club?* The whole thing struck Kalee as very unfair. Her gyrations grew faster and faster the more she thought about it.

"Ow!" said John, face muffled by Kalee's cleavage.

Kalee stopped moving. "What's the matter, baby?" she cooed.

"G'off, g'off me."

Kalee stepped back from John. He clapped a hand over his nose, protectively.

"What happened? What's wrong?" she asked.

John moved his hand away from his nose. Kalee realized the rim of John's left nostril was bleeding from a tiny slit. She had managed to nick him with one of the sequins on her push-up bra. *Oh shit, not again.*

"John, I'm so sorry. Let me get the first aid kit, I'll fix you," Kalee said. She started walking toward the bar.

"No, it's ok, darlin', I'm ok, just come back 'n dance some more," John said, dabbing at his nose with a paper napkin from the dispenser on the table.

Kalee continued toward the bar anyway. Pete, the manager at Club Vee, had been furious the last time she'd accidentally cut a customer on her sequined bra.

"Kalee, this is a vegan club!" he'd screamed. "It's important that the club stay one hundred percent blood-free at all times. We can't be getting any blood on the floor or in the drains or anything!"

Kalee had not been intimidated by Pete's outburst. "The customers aren't going to be licking the floor or the drains, are they? Why does it matter?" she asked.

Fuming, Pete had grumbled, "It just does, ok? We were really lucky this time, even though the guy got cut, we kept it contained, so we're all right. Next time we might not be so lucky."

"But the blood isn't going into the food, so who cares? I just don't get it," Kalee said, shrugging her bronzed and glitter-gelled shoulders.

Pete had sighed heavily, and taken a deep breath to calm himself. "Consider it a matter of principle, Kalee. It's essential to our business model. Besides, you benefit from the policy—that's why all you dancers get time off with pay when you get your monthlies," he had argued.

Kalee had thought it over at the time, and because she liked the paid time-off, she didn't object further. *Every workplace has a few weird rules, I wonder if he's blood-phobic? I think that's called homophobia. Should remember to look that up on my phone when I'm on break.* Kalee pushed those thoughts aside. *I dunno what Pete is gonna do with another sequin incident. He's gonna ban this costume for sure, it's a two-time offender.* She looked down at the green and red sequined bra she was wearing. *This is my best holiday season costume. If he bans it, what else can I wear that's festive?*

Kalee was damned if she'd do what some of the other dancers did—wear Santa or elf hats while they danced. Kalee considered herself an artist, and her costumes were an integral part of that. *I guess I have the silver lamé one, I could maybe get some glitter stick-on tattoos that look like snowflakes, maybe do a Jack Frost theme.*

When she reached the bar she told Amber, the bartender, that she needed the first aid kit.

"How come? You didn't cut yourself, did you?" asked Amber with alarm. Amber dug a hair elastic out of the front pocket of her jeans, and started to put her long red hair into a pony tail.

"No, not me. I nicked John's nose with a sequin," Kalee explained.

Worry flashed over Amber's face like gathering storm clouds. "Oh shit," she said, looking over Kalee's shoulder at John on the other side of the room.

"What? Is Pete out here walking around checking on us?" asked Kalee.

Staring at John, Amber said, "No, I think he's gonna knock those bloody tissues off the table with his elbow. JOHN –NOOOO BE CAREFUL WITH THOSE TISSUES!"

John turned his head to look at Amber. He looked at her quizzically and shrugged. His elbow hit a crumpled bloody tissue, and it fell to the floor.

Kalee could hear a scream from Pete's office. The club patrons and dancers went silent. Rick the DJ, one headphone held against his ear, pressed 'pause' on his equipment. The silence was deafening. The manager's office door flung open violently, and Pete stood in the doorway, his chest heaving and his eyes wild.

"Amber!" he shouted, "There is blood on the floor, I feel it!"

"I'm on it!" she shouted back. Amber ducked behind the bar and pulled out a sawed-off shotgun. Even cut down, the shot gun was almost as long as Amber's short arms. She moved the slide on the gun, loading shells into the chamber. The sound of the gun cocking drew all eyes to Amber. Several men stood up slowly from their tables and started to edge their way to the exit. The dancer on stage slowly backed up to duck behind the stage curtains.

"Take this," Amber said to Kalee, handing her the shotgun over the bar. "You're going to need it. Take off your stupid platform shoes, too— you are tall enough to aim for their heads without them," barked Amber.

"Their heads?"

"Yes, aim for their fucking heads, bitch. Now take off your shoes."

Kalee stepped out of her high-heeled clear acrylic mules. Flat-footed, she stood about five foot seven, six inches taller than Amber.

Amber ducked down behind the bar again and came back up with a sword. *Why the fuck does she have a sword back there?* Placing a hand on the polished wood of the bar top, Amber vaulted over the bar, and landed on the balls of her feet next to Kalee. Kalee gaped at her. *I had no idea Amber knew parkour.*

"Pete," Amber shouted, "Get the herbs ready!"

Kalee was about to ask Amber what was going on when the floor started to rock and buck under their feet.

Kalee could hear the customers and dancers behind her yelling and running around. She grabbed Amber's shoulder before Amber could bolt away. "What the hell is going on? Is this an earthquake? Who am I supposed to shoot? I don't want to kill customers!" screamed Kalee, above the din.

Amber's blue eyes flashed like shards of pitiless glass. "Not customers, dummy, the restless dead! Turn around and look!" Amber shoved Kalee's shoulder to make her turn around.

Sections of the concrete floor were rippling and buckling, coming away in chunks. It was as if a mole of monstrous size was burrowing just under the floor of Club Vee. Kalee watched in shock as two hands appeared, digging their way out of a nearby pile of concrete rubble. The hands were tinged green from mold, and a tar-like black ichor oozed from under the broken fingernails. The tendons in the hands tensed, and Kalee looked on in horror as the dead man pulled himself up through the hole he had made. He was still buried from the waist down, and seemed to be gathering his energies to climb out of the earth the rest of the way. His face was not much more than strings of rotted meat, but his eyes blinked, and settled on Amber and Kalee. He started to snarl and growl, hands scrabbling for purchase in the rubble.

Lithe and catlike, Amber sprang forward toward him, holding her sword in a two-handed grip. Leading with her left arm, she swung the blade. It made a sickening wet *splurk* as it bit into the dead man's neck and severed his head from his body. The head rolled away. It splattered sticky ichor from the ragged end of the neck over the concrete debris. The eyes were open and blinking, and he was still snarling and gnashing his teeth. The smell of sulphur and putrefaction permeated the nightclub. Kalee's stomach rolled and twisted with nausea. *I shouldn't have had that cauliflower tagine.*

Kalee felt her mind start to retreat from what she was seeing, trivialities rushing in to fill the available brain-space. *I wonder how long Amber has used a sword? Maybe that's what she does on her nights off. It explains the muscle definition in her arms . . .SLAP!*

Kalee's hand flew to her burning cheek. "You hit me!" she yelled at Amber.

"Yes, and I'll do it again before I let you stand here and get chewed on by these dinks. You have a gun, so fucking use it," Amber growled.

"These are zombies?" asked Kalee

Amber rolled her eyes, and ran toward Pete's office. She dodged a tall man who in life must have weighed at least three hundred pounds. Amber swung her blade at him, but he dodged. The large dead man kept his head, but lost his left arm. Amber kept moving towards Pete's office.

Kalee saw the fingers on the hand of the severed arm bend and flex. The hand started to crawl toward Kalee, dragging the arm behind it, trailing noodle-like tendons and the stench of the grave.

Kalee's face settled into grim lines. "Your fingers are not gonna do the walking today, buddy," she said.

She raised the shotgun to shoulder level and pulled the trigger. The fat man's head exploded in a fountain of green mold and black ichor. The arm stopped moving. *Holy shit. Not only am I a great shot, apparently I have mad skillz with action hero one-liners.*

Feeling more confident, Kalee cocked the shotgun again. She looked around the club.

Rick the DJ had, so far, managed to fend off the zombies who approached his platform. Barricaded behind his sound equipment, he had a vinyl record in each hand. His dark skin gleamed with sweat as he used the edge as a slashing weapon. Any zombies who had gotten close had at least a few slashes across their rotted cheeks and hands.

A few more zombies shambled aimlessly across the club's floor, bumping into tables and knocking over chairs. They sniffed the air, searching for scents. *Looks like they're trying to find someone to chase.* Kalee noticed that most of the customers and workers seemed to have made it out of the club before the dead had gotten free enough of the earth to grab or bite anyone. *Maybe they're following the scent of the people that left, that'd be the strongest smell, right?*

John had not been one of the patrons lucky enough to escape the club. His body was bent backwards over a small table, entrails hanging down to the floor on either side. A dead woman and her two small dead children were red to the elbows with John's blood as they feasted on his organs. Kalee could hear the wet smacking sounds they made as they ate. The smaller of the children, a little girl with blue mold and phosphorescent fungus growing in her once-blonde pigtails, made a low hoarse groaning sound in her throat as she chewed and swallowed.

Kalee sighted on the middle of their mother's forehead and pulled the trigger. *Headshot!* Neither of the children looked up from their buffet. She re-loaded quickly and shot the brother, blowing off the lower half of his jaw. *That might be good enough, he can't really bite anybody without his jaw.* The dead boy continued to shove handfuls of John's liver into what was left of his mouth. He looked perplexed. *I guess he hasn't figured it out he can't chew.*

Kalee ran toward the DJ platform, skirting the occupied child zombies, and leapt over piles of broken concrete and churned earth. Kalee was amazed at her own agility. *All those hours swinging by my knee from a brass pole are really paying off.*

Two zombies, a man and a woman, were pressed against the DJ equipment, arms waving as they reached out to grab Rick. Rick darted forward, surprisingly quick for a large man, and slashed at their hands and faces with two vinyl records. Black ichor splattered the equipment. The zombies seemed impervious to pain. Rick jumped back, out of the way of their desperate grasping hands.

Kalee stopped about five feet behind the zombies, chambered a round, and lifted the shotgun to her shoulder, sighting the back of one of the zombies' heads. At the time the man had died, he head had been newly-shaved. The back of his head sported a black spider web tattoo. *It's like a bullseye.*

BAM. The recoil rocked Kalee's stance, and she noticed her shoulder was getting tender from where the butt of the gun slammed against it.

The bald zombie staggered for a minute. Headless, he fell forward into the DJ equipment. Lana Del Ray's "Fucked My Way to the Top" started to boom through the club's speakers. *LIFE IS AWESOME, I CONFESS. WHAT I DO, I DO BEST.*

"Rick," Kalee shouted, "I got you. Run to the office!" Rick looked at her with eyes showing too much white. Kalee chambered another round. Rick looked around, waiting for his chance.

The petite female zombie menacing the DJ platform turned around at the sound of the shotgun chambering the shell. Rick tipped a speaker the size of a refrigerator over on its side, and bolted for the office door. The music continued to wail. I FUCKED MY WAY UP TO THE TOP. GO, BABY, GO, GO, GO, GO, GO . . .

Unlike the other zombies Kalee had seen, this one had very little rot. The others had been mindless eating machines trailing shredded flesh. This girl was different; she had a gleam of cunning in her eye and most of her still-pretty face was intact. She had an upturned snub nose and Cupid's bow lips. She snarled at Kalee. Kalee pulled the trigger. Her shot grazed the small zombie's shoulder. *Oh shit.*

The zombie lunged forward and tried to grab Kalee's arm. Kalee stumbled backward, tripping over concrete rubble. She landed hard on her tailbone, rough chunks of debris tearing the soft skin of Kalee's buttocks as she hit the floor. She had managed to keep a hold on the sawed-off shotgun.

The zombie rushed Kalee, impossibly fast, mouth foaming. *Fuck fuck fuck.* Lana Del Rey's recorded voice continued to whisper and wail: LAY ME DOWN TONIGHT, IN MY DIAMONDS AND PEARLS. TELL ME SONGS AT NIGHT, ABOUT YOUR FAVORITE GIRL.

Kalee gripped the gun at either end. She used it to keep the zombie's snapping teeth away from her face. Even though the girl was not as rotted as they others, she reeked of meat and embalming chemicals. Kalee felt herself gag. The zombie was unnaturally strong. Kalee's arms shook with the effort of keeping the zombie away from her face and throat. *She's gonna rip my face off.* The zombie was close enough that her foaming saliva dripped on Kalee's face. Kalee turned her head and squeezed her eyes shut. I'M A DRAGON, YOU'RE A WHORE, DON'T EVEN KNOW WHAT YOU'RE GOOD FOR.

A wet *splorch* made her open her eyes. Rick stood over her, the back of a chair gripped in his massive hands. He had used the chair to bat the zombie off of Kalee. She looked at him in amazement.

"Supernatural they might be," he said philosophically, "but physics is physics." He grinned under his beard. He grabbed Kalee under the arm pit, and dragged her to her feet.

They ran to the manager's office at the back of the club. The jawless boy stood ankle deep in the gore that had been his sister and mother, puzzling over the fact he could no longer chew. The rest of the zombies seemed to have found the exits, and were presumably milling around the parking lot or wandering across I-5.

Kalee hammered on the door. "Pete! Open up!"

"How do I know you're not a zombie?" said Pete, from the other side of the door.

Kalee could hear Amber in the background saying "Don't be an idiot, Pete, let Kalee in here."

"But what if it's a trick, and she eats us?" whined Pete.

Rick stepped forward, slamming the thin door with his fist. "Be worried about me, motherfucker, Imma eat you whether I'm a zombie or not."

The locked clicked open, and Amber opened the door a crack.

"No bites?" she asked, eyeing Kalee and Rick.

"Not yet," said Kalee.

"Ok, come in." Amber stepped back, and Rick and Kalee slipped into the office.

Pete was crumpled on the floor, his face a mask of pain. His hands clutched at his groin.

Kalee pointed her chin at Pete. "What's with him?"

"I had to nail him in the balls to get him to open to the door,"

"Nice," said Rick, teeth flashing white. He kicked Pete in the ribs. "And that's for building the club on an ancient burial ground, AGAIN".

"Again?" asked Kalee.

Amber sighed, and rubbed her eyes with the thumb and fingers of her left hand. "That's why we had to leave Missouri and come to Oregon."

"This has happened before?!" Kalee face-palmed.

Rick kicked Pete again. Pete groaned, and rolled away from him, hiding his face. "Stupid motherfucker leased the land cheap in Missouri, but the same thing happened there on Surf n' Turf Saturday." Rick scowled, and sat on the edge of Pete's desk.

"So you guys thought a vegan club would prevent it," asked Kalee.

Amber shrugged and shook her head. Pete sat up, hands clutching his bruised ribs now. "It would have worked it you weren't so fucking clumsy, you stupid bitch."

Kalee considered hitting Pete with the butt of the sawed off shotgun, but while she was weighing the pros and cons, Amber said, "Pete, shut up. You're only making it worse."

"Worse?! How can it be worse?" Pete yelled. "The fucking restless dead are roaming I-5! Do you know how much money we're gonna have to give the cops to keep this quiet? It'll break us."

"It'll break you," said Amber quietly.

"What do you mean by that?"

"After Missouri, I told you that if things got fucked up in Portland, I was gone. Consider this my notice," said Amber.

"Me, too," said Rick, glowering.

Kalee had a thought. "Have you guys ever thought about starting a club in maybe Mexico or something? I have dual citizenship."

Amber raised an eyebrow, and Pete started to cry. Kalee could hear the wail of emergency sirens over the Lana Del Ray song.

The next week *The Portland Voice* ran the following article:

> Local authorities in Portland vowed Monday to prosecute the perpetrators of the violent disturbances that took place last Wednesday night at Club Vee, Portland's premiere vegan adult entertainment club. A winter solstice 'buy one, get one' sale on lap dances led to rioting, which resulted in property damage, dozens of arrests and injuries, and the tragic death of Portland clergyman, John Ryerson.
>
> Three staff members—Amber Boucher, Kalee Rodriguez, and Richard Jackson— are still being sought for questioning about the brawl. Portland Police Media Coordinator Kenneth Whiteside said that while the three staff members "did nothing criminal," they did "exercise poor judgment"

during the melee on Wednesday.

Witnesses have suggested that the vegan buffet may have been spiked with PCP or so-called 'bath salts' because of the level of bizarre violence during the riot.

Mrs. Janice Ryerson, Pastor Ryerson's wife, stated that "he was always ministering to all kinds of people; he didn't judge. It's tragic that in trying to save the souls of these degraded girls in the club, he met his own death. But he's with Jesus now."

Services for Pastor Ryerson will be held on Saturday at Church of Christ, Crucified on Templeton Avenue. The family has asked that in lieu of flowers, people wishing to pay their respects to Pastor Ryerson make donations to the girl's scholarship fund established to honour his name.

Where Did This Box Come From?

Author's note: *Lest you believe I only ever complain to customer service, let me set you straight. Like many writers, I have done many different kinds of work in order to make ends meet, writing being—thus far, anyway—about as lucrative as selling woven friendship bracelets from a stand outside the art museum. So one of the many jobs I've held in my life so far has been that of a logistics/customer service agent. In other words, I have been the complainee far more often than I have been the complainer.*

Transcript of <online furniture retailer> Logistics/Customer Service Call, December 15 2015:

Chloe: Welcome to <redacted> Logistics and Customer Service. You're speaking with Chloe. How can I help?

Male Caller: Where did this box come from?

Chloe: Pardon me, sir?

Male Caller: Are you stupid? I want to know why you sent me this box!

Chloe: Hhm, ok, let's try to find out what is going on. Can I get your name and address?

Male Caller: <gives personal information as requested>

Chloe: I'm sorry, sir, I can't seem to find your name or address in the database. Is there perhaps another name or address that was used in the order?

Male Caller: How would I know? You're the one that sent it!

Chloe: Hmm, might someone have ordered you a Christmas present and had it delivered to your home without you knowing it was coming?

Male Caller: How the hell would I know?

Chloe: Ok, just trying to think of some possibilities of how that box got on your porch even though you didn't order it . . .

Male Caller: Well the UPS man just brought it and left it on my porch. He didn't ring the bell or anything. He just put this huge stupid box on my porch without my permission and drove away.

Chloe: Oh dear, that sounds very annoying. What does the shipping label say? [Chloe Google-maps physical address the man gave. The search returns a map of rural Missouri so remote, there are no street-view pictures].

Male Caller: I don't know.

Chloe: Would it be possible to have a look at it and tell me what it says?

Male Caller: No way I'm touching that thing.

Chloe [mutes mic on headset and sighs. Co-workers look over at her with raised eyebrows. Chloe nods, then unmutes mic]: Well, I'm trying to help you figure out what this box is doing on your porch. If it's a mistake, I can help get the box re-routed to wherever it was supposed to go. Maybe you could take a photo of it with your phone and send it to me in email?

Male Caller: [shouting] I don't know anything about that. I'm an old man, I can't be fooling around with email and such. [Caller drops the phone on a hard surface. Caller can be heard yelling at another person in his home. Sound of stomping feet.]

Female Caller: Why are you giving my father a hard time?

Chloe: [instant messages shift supervisor about problem call, supervisor starts to listen in for QA purposes]: Pardon me, ma'am?

Female Caller: Some jackass from UPS put this box on my father's porch and we want it gone!

Chloe: I can definitely help you with that, but I need to know what the shipping label on the box says.

Female Caller: I'm not touching that effing box.

Chloe: Just so I understand, may I ask why you can't touch the box?

Female Caller: Anthrax, you dummy!

Chloe: Hmm, so what you're saying is you think UPS left a box contaminated with anthrax on your father's porch?

Female Caller: Did you take your stupid pills this morning? Not UPS, ISIS!

Chloe: [mutes mic on headset, face palms. Supervisor listening in falls out of her chair as she is laughing so hard. Chloe unmutes mic] Ok, let me see if I've understood what you are telling me. You are saying that an ISIS terrorist, dressed as a UPS delivery man, left a large, unwanted box that might be contaminated with anthrax on your dad's porch, is that right?

Female Caller: Yes.

Chloe: And so you have called me hoping that <redacted> Logistics & Customer Service can help you with the disposal of this box?

Female Caller: Yes, exactly.

Chloe: Well, I would like to help you get rid of the box. Maybe you could look at the box without touching it and tell me what the shipping label says?

Female Caller: No way I'm opening the door, there could be a bomb in there, too, along with anthrax.

Chloe: Ummm, maybe the people to call would be the police?

Female Caller: [shouting into phone] We already tried that!

Chloe: [pinching bridge of nose to fend off tension headache] Ok, and what did they say?

Female Caller: They said that we should call the 1-800 number on the box and tell you guys to come get it.

Chloe: And that's why you are calling <redacted> logistics & customer service?

Female Caller: No, we're calling you because Walmart said to call you.

Chloe: So the box has Walmart markings on it?

Female Caller: No, but we figured to try them first.

Chloe: I see. [Supervisor makes throat-cutting gesture to Chloe, indicating Chloe should terminate the call]

Female Caller: So you'll send someone to get this thing outta here?

Chloe: Unfortunately, I won't be able to do that, ma'am. My supervisor has asked me to end this call.

Female Caller: Wait! I need to know one thing!

Chloe: What is that?

Female Caller: Can you give me the number for Amazon customer service?

Chloe: [disconnects call].

Feed Me

The apartment was full of delicious smells. But whenever I jumped up on the counter to see exactly what the Big Monkey Thing was doing to the food, she shooed me away. I begged for a sample—meowing, circling her ankles, stretching up as far as I could reach to tap her on the hip with a soft paw—but she ignored me.

I found Small Cat sleeping in the middle of the bed, and chewed her ear until she woke.

Small Cat hissed at me, but followed me back to the kitchen. I continued to beg Big Monkey Thing for meat from my position on the floor, while Small Cat walked across the counter, investigating the contents of the sink.

She's peeling vegetables right now, said Small Cat, through our psychic link.

Ugh. Hate those. I paused in my begging and meowing, and composed myself, tail wrapped politely to the left.

You hate everything.

I find Small Cat to be a little judgmental. Truth be told, I think she's obnoxious, but as companions go, she's not the worst one I've had. Fat Cat used to live with us, and she was grumpy all the time and wouldn't come out from under the bed. Definitely an Only-Cat, that one.

The meat smell is coming from any empty pan, said Small Cat, *looks like she took all the meat out and now the pan is in the sink, half-full of water.*

I leapt to the counter to see what Small Cat was describing. Big Monkey Thing said something in her language to us. Small Cat was too busy drinking meat-water to pay any attention. I myself try not to listen to Big Monkey Thing's language, it gets on my nerves.

Try the meat-water, said Small Cat, *it's delicious.*

Don't mind if I do. I lapped at the meat-water from the opposite side of the sink.

The Other Big Monkey Thing- the calm, male one- came into the apartment with some paper bags. Bringing home more food?

Yay, he's home, squealed Small Cat. She jumped from her sink-side position onto Other Big Monkey Thing's shoulder and started to purr.

Small Cat is a real brown-noser, always sucking up to Other Big Monkey Thing.

Monkey Thing said something in her language to Other Big Monkey Thing. He scooped me up in his arms—I hate that—and carried me to the bedroom while Small Cat rode his shoulder.

In the bedroom, Other Monkey Thing made the magic happen. A red dot appeared and started moving across the carpet. Small Cat and I have never caught the elusive red dot, but I think we will, one day. If Fat Cat was still around, her help might have made all the difference.

Eventually Other Monkey Thing grew bored of making magic for us. He stretched out on the bed. Small Cat nestled against his left hip, so I settled into his right armpit. We slept.

When I woke up, Other Monkey Thing was still asleep. I decided to fix that. I tapped Other Monkey Thing's nose with my paw. He twitched, and rolled away onto his side.

Hey Small Cat

Playing with string right now

I need your help with Other Monkey Thing

Busy!

Come on, he won't wake up

Did you tap his nose with your paw?

Yes, I did, it didn't work. Your floof should do the trick.

I just have to do everything around here, don't I?

See what I mean? Small Cat is persnickety, even on one of her good days. She sauntered into the bedroom, narrowed her eyes at me, and jumped up on the bed. She draped herself over Other Monkey Thing's head like a fluffy cap and curled her magnificent plumed tail over his face.

Soon Other Monkey Thing started to snort and sneeze. Small Cat's fur gets him every time.

He moaned something in his language, but opened his eyes. I bit his wrist, not puncturing the skin, just showing him the love. He likes it when I play-bite him, I just know it. It always makes him get out of bed. It's a game we play.

Play-biting is also my signal to him that the food bowl is only half-full. Food bowls should always be full. I don't know about you, but I get very uncomfortable when I can see the bottom of the bowl peeking out from underneath the crunchy kibble. Life would be easier if monkey-things could communicate psychically like we cats do, but one must make allowances for their limitations. No psychic links with other animals, mostly fur-less, have to clean themselves with WATER (how disgusting is that?)

I do my best to communicate with my monkey-things on their level.

"MEOWWWWW!" I screamed.

Whoa, said Small Cat. *Maybe you could be a little louder? Will that make him smarter all of a sudden?*

Don't be sour, Small Cat, I'm just trying to get him to fill up the bowl. If I don't make noise, he might forget, and then we'll run out of food.

Yeah, well, you could stand to miss a meal or two, fatty.

Small Cat! Don't be mean!

Phhhft! she replied, and then crawled under the bed to stand guard over all her stolen treasures.

Small Cat is something of a klepto— she likes to steal wine corks, thumb drives, anything small that she can drag under the bed into her lair.

Honestly, I think Small Cat— with her crotchety attitude and penchant for gloating over her purloined baubles— must have been a dragon in a past life. What she must have done to get promoted to cat in this incarnation boggles the mind.

Other Monkey Thing was taking his time grabbing the cat food bag from the pantry and filling the bowl, so I yowled a few more times, just to make sure he got the point.

Other Monkey Thing said something like, "Blah blah blah, Tux, blah blah blah blabbity blah blah."

Both of my monkey things are under the impression that my name is "Tux" because of my glorious shiny black and white fur. Like I said, they are idiots. But they are my idiots, and I love them, even if I have to holler to get basic food service around this place.

The Drunk Parrot: A Modern Fable

Not too long ago, quite close to this place, a mother and her adult son lived in a high-rise called Plaza Pointe. They each occupied their own separate one-bedroom apartment on the first floor. Astrid had moved to Plaza Pointe after her divorce back in 2001. When the only other apartment on her floor came up for sale a few years later, Stan—with some help from Astrid— purchased it. Their apartments were separated from the lobby, mailboxes, and other common spaces by a sturdy metal door that could only be opened with an electronic fob. As the high rise was located mid-way up a steep hill, their first-floor apartment balconies jutted out over the parking lot of the adjacent mall and afforded a scenic panorama. Mother and son had seclusion with a southward, river-facing view.

Stan appreciated having just one near neighbour, for he had a checkered history of eviction. There had been frequent complaints from neighbours about noise and raucous parties. Landlords endured damage to their suites and non-payment of rent. Stan knew his mother Astrid was unlikely to complain about anything he did. He knew that if he was running short of money because the casinos or the bars had beckoned, she would help him out. Astrid was always helping Stan.

Astrid derived peace of mind from the extra sound proofing because of Peaches. Peaches was a snowy-white cockatoo of prodigious size and indeterminate age. He was fond of cursing loudly in German. Astrid surmised Peaches' German-speaking former owners had a tempestuous relationship. Peaches could (and frequently did) make sounds that would fool the uninitiated into thinking that someone was slowly skinning a weasel alive while an entire ward's worth of colicky babies cried inconsolably. Peaches' companionship was an acquired taste.

Astrid inherited Peaches when she purchased a family-run pet store with some of the proceeds from her divorce. She would not have chosen such a pet but she wanted to be her own boss, and the location was just steps from her front door. The former owners were adamant that they wouldn't sell unless the buyer promised to care for Peaches. On the day Astrid picked up the keys to the store, the former owner told her "If vee ever find you haf sent Peaches to zee glue factory, vee will sue you!"

Peaches was better company than she had anticipated, so his tenure in *Astrid's Pet Emporium* was secure. It had never really been in danger, despite his swearing and squawking. Astrid was tender-hearted. And so it went: Astrid and Peaches presided over the tiny pet store in Columbia Square for the next seventeen years. When the sun was out, business was brisk, and Peaches ate cashews from her hand, Astrid had never been happier.

That came to an end in the fall of 2018. Astrid was forced into retirement. Her small store could no longer compete with the big-box pet stores. She was forced to sell her shop to Pet-co. They declined her offer to stay on as manager. Pet-co wanted to sell frozen raw meat to dog-owning Millennials. Their young, glossy social media manager told sixty-eight-year-old Astrid that she was "not a good fit for our brand or the Pet-co lifestyle". Pet-co was adamant that when Astrid left, Peaches go with her.

Astrid was pleased they didn't want to keep Peaches. She liked to complain about her bird, but she loved him.

During her first few months of retirement, Astrid made ends meet with ease. She even contemplated taking a vacation somewhere sunny. But before she could buy a plane ticket, Stan asked for help. He was almost a year in arrears with his strata fees, and had missed a couple of mortgage payments besides. Fines were piling up on top of his arrears. Could Astrid help him with his money problems? She did, after all, have the small nest egg left from the sale of the store. Astrid reluctantly wrote him a cheque. She thought, *Once a mother, always a mother, I guess.*

The month after that Stan needed financial help with his car repairs—something had gone wrong with the transmission in his truck. Astrid wrote another cheque. The following month Stan had some trouble paying his phone bill and apparently needed a brand-new Iphone as well. Astrid wrote another cheque. Six months after Astrid retired, her nest egg was gone.

Without her financial cushion, Astrid found there was consistently more month than there was pension cheque. Her years as a homemaker and small business owner meant that her pension was not robust. Astrid did as many seniors do; she got a part-time job to supplement her income. This arrangement suited her well enough.

It did not suit Peaches. He was used to Astrid's companionship throughout the day, so being alone in the apartment for hours at a stretch was not something he relished.

After her first day of work, frustrated Peaches spent the evening nipping Astrid while perched on the arm of the couch. He bobbed and squawked as she tried to watch TV. Even after she turned it off and indulged in her nightly ritual of reading in bed, Peaches kept fussing. Eventually she had to put him in his cage and cover it with a blanket to encourage him to sleep. Peaches kept muttering *svinehund* from beneath the cage cover. Eventually he was quiet enough that Astrid could ignore him and finally fall asleep.

After work on her second day, Astrid came home to find that Peaches had destroyed one of the kitchen chairs. In his anxiety and boredom he had used his hard beak to reduce a wooden captain's chair to a pile of splintered rubble.

Astrid knelt to sweep up the remains of the chair. She could not afford the expense of parrot daycare— *if such a service even exists in New Westminster. I've seen places like that for dogs, but none for birds. Besides, dog-daycare is almost as expensive as child-*

daycare. That would make my working pointless if it takes my whole pay cheque to pay for Peaches to go to daycare. Astrid's mind raced. *Could I take him to work with me? Would Walmart let me have Peaches on my shoulder as I greet customers? Maybe I could sew him a little matching vest so that he was properly in uniform?* She entertained a mental image of Peaches in a tiny quilted vest, distributing complimentary handi-wipes to the germaphobes too precious to touch shopping cart handles. That made her smile. *They'll never let me, though, I just know it.*

Astrid finished sweeping up the bits of wood, and leaned back to ease her aching L-spine. *I can't come home to this every day.*

She checked out a copy of *Parrots for Dummies* from the public library in the hopes it had suggestions for bored birds. It didn't offer anything Astrid hadn't already thought of.

Out of options, Astrid decided she would ask Stan for help. She was aware her forty-year-old son had certain . . . limitations. *But I think all of that is in the past now. He holds down a full-time job and everything. It's going to be ok, I'm certain of it.*

Astrid knocked on Stan's door.

"Can you bird-sit for me?"

"Sure, Mum, when?"

Astrid hesitated. "Er, I need someone with him for a while every day that I work."

Stan rolled his eyes. "That much? Why? What's wrong with him?"

"Well, he's not used to being alone and he doesn't like it."

"So? He'll get over it."

"You should go look in my garbage can and see what he did."

"What did he do?"

"He ate one of the kitchen chairs."

Stan laughed, but when Astrid didn't, he walked down their short shared hallway and into her apartment.

"Holy shit, Mum, that's nuts!"

Astrid burst into tears.

"Hey, hey, it's ok, I'll do it, ok? Don't cry!"

Stan agreed to eat lunch in Astrid's place three days a week. Since he worked in the Columbia Square liquor store, almost as close to Plaza Pointe as Astrid's former pet store, it was easy to slip away for lunch. Astrid hoped that would be enough to keep Peaches entertained.

From the first day Stan had lunch-duty with the large bird, Peaches' acts of household vandalism stopped. Astrid was certain this was because Peaches enjoyed Stan's company. She imagined Stan playing games with Peaches, tempting him with interesting toys to puzzle over.

She was mistaken. Peaches stopped creating sawdust from the household furnishings because Stan fed him Skittles and sips of Mike's Hard Lemonade every day for lunch.

It all started the first day Stan ate lunch at Astrid's. He chewed his baloney sandwich and watched the Arabic language news on the community access station with the English captions turned on. Peaches watched, too, bobbing with the language-rhythms. Stan was trying to learn a few Arabic phrases because he wanted to impress a pretty Arabic-speaking girl who worked at the local movie theatre.

"Hey, buddy, you like that?"

"As-salām alaykum." [1]

"That's pretty good for a bird!"

As Stan worked his mouth around Arabic syllables, he flicked Skittles for Peaches to snap out of the air. He cracked open a third Mike's Hard lemonade,

---

1 "Hello"; literally "peace be unto you"

Original Flavour, and ran Peaches around the living room with the laser pointer. Peaches never tired of chasing the tiny red spot.

On this day, thought, Peaches was more attracted to the fruity aromas coming from the long-necked glass bottle. He flap-hopped onto the arm of the couch next to Stan.

"You thirsty, little guy?"

"As-salām alaykum," replied Peaches.

"I'll take that as a yes," said Stan, as he titled the bottle.

Peaches slurped the last few centimeters of the beverage.

This became their routine. Sandwich, Skittles, Arabic TV, Mike's Hard Lemonade. Then a few laps around the coffee table with the laser pointer until Peaches collapsed on the carpet muttering *svinehund* and *as-salām alaykum*. Usually he put a wing over his head and starting to snore before Stan returned to work.

Astrid arrived home after work to a very thirsty bird. As she was filling the bird's water cup for a third time, she wondered, *Is he giving Peaches scraps of sandwich meat as a treat? I should tell him not to do that. Surely all that salt isn't good for a bird, it makes him so thirsty.* She re-filled Peaches' seed cup. *On the other hand, he's not making kindling of the furniture, the couch cushions are unmolested, and it seems like he's in good spirits.* Astrid donned disposable latex gloves and removed the soiled newspaper at the bottom of the cage. *I wonder what the Arabic is all about?* She laid out several layers of clean newspaper. *Ah, not important.* She discarded the soiled newspaper, peeled off the gloves, and chucked them in the bin. *If Peaches is happy, I'm happy.* Astrid washed her hands at the kitchen sink and dried them on a tea towel. *Maybe things can get back to normal around here and I can relax.* She settled onto the couch with Peaches on her shoulder. She stroked the bird's feathered head, and turned the TV to a re-run of *NCIS*.

"This is the life, hey Peachy-boy?"

"As-salām alaykum."

About eight weeks into their arrangement, Astrid had the opportunity to go on an overnight visit to the Sunshine Coast to see her cousin. There was no question of taking Peaches: Astrid's cousin had terrible allergies to any kind of bird or animal dander. Stan offered to stay in his mother's apartment while she was away to care for the bird. He even drove Astrid to the terminal to catch the ferry.

When Stan returned home, he assembled a few supplies he would need while bird-sitting: Costco sized bag of skittles . . . CHECK. Five four-packs of Mike's Hard Lemonade, Original Flavour? CHECK. Laptop computer so he could watch and listen to Arabic-language videos on You Tube? CHECK. Oh, and since it was the weekend and because Astrid had a gas barbeque on her balcony, Stan brought two seven hundred-and-fifty ml bottles of Johnny Walker Red and a package of chicken hot dogs.

By eight pm on the Saturday night, both Stan and Peaches were rollicking drunk. Stan sang off-key renditions of Rhianna songs. Peaches screeched *as-salām 'alaykum* and *svinehund* at ear-shredding volume.

When Stan laid himself out on the living room carpet to dissuade the room from spinning, Peaches hopped onto Stan's chest, peered into his face, and whispered, "Sohn einer hündin,[2] flachwichser!"[3]

Stan kept his eyes closed. "Ok, buddy, ok, I get it, you want some supper."

Stan wobbled his way out to the balcony with a long-handled roasting fork, the package of hot dogs, and a small box of wooden matches. He knew that the auto-light feature on his mother's barbeque hadn't worked for years. To light the gas, you had to hold a lit match near the jets underneath the lava rocks at the bottom of the barbeque.

Stan, unsteady, pulled one of Astrid's balcony chairs close. He would sit while he roasted the meat.

---

[2] Son-of-a-bitch
[3] Motherfucker

The grill was still sticky and crusted from last night, when he'd barbequed ribs. There was lots of ebonized crud stuck to the grill, so it was easier to use the roasting fork. *I'll clean the grill before Mum gets home,* he thought, then immediately forgot about it.

He impaled a couple of hot dogs on the tines of the roasting fork, and leaned it, pointy-end up, against the balcony table. He hunched over and turned the valve on the propane tank. He knew you had to wait for a few moment, so that enough gas had come out of the jets to actually get ignition.

Peaches squawked from inside.

"I hear you, man. It's not just inside that's spinning, it's outside, too." Stan's consonants sounded wet and misshapen. He rested his head against the closed lid of the barbeque. His eyes closed. Minutes passed.

He started awake, roused by the smell of propane. *Keep it together man, you don't want to blow yourself up.* He scraped the head of the wooden match against his thumbnail, and held it near the propane jets. The gas that had accumulated under the closed lid of the barbeque exploded. The lid lifted ten centimeters, and flames shot out in all directions.

Stan toppled over sideways, trying to avoid the flames. His legs were tangled in the balcony chair. His head bounced like an overripe melon on the concrete floor of the balcony.

He laid still, blinking, trying to get his bearings. *My clothes are singed, but I don't think I'm burned.* He noticed that the woven outdoor mat was smoldering in places, but was not actually on fire. *Hafta stomp that out.* He noticed that Astrid's long floral curtains had escaped harm. *That's good. Mum'll be pissed if I mess up her stuff.*

Stan got to his feet slowly, touching the wetness at his temple. *Blood,* he thought, looking at his fingers. Everything was spinning around him. *Even the stars have tracers following them, like that time I dropped acid in the tenth grade. I wonder if . . .*

Drunk, head-injured, and slightly singed, Stan tripped over his own feet and fell forward onto the roasting fork. The tines pierced his left eye, and then deeper, into his brain. He was dead before the hotdogs fell off the tines.

Curious, Peaches hopped out to the balcony to investigate. Stan was not moving.

Peaches said, "Bil-hanā' wa ash-shifā" [4] and—standing in an ever-deepening puddle of Stan's blood—ate one of the fallen hot dogs.

Peaches peered into Stan's slack, blood-coated face and shrieked.

---

4 Bon appetit! Literally "May you have your meal with gladness and health."

No response from Stan. The bird cocked his head, considering the situation.

Peaches ate the second hot dog.

By the time first responders arrived—people in the parking lot below had heard the explosion of the barbeque—Peaches had plucked Stan's uninjured eye from its socket. It dangled from his beak as he tried to evade capture.

One of the EMTs herded Peaches from the balcony back into the living room, but Peaches would not surrender his gelatinous prize.

Peaches half-ran, half-flapped all over the room, leaving bloody bird footprints all over the beige carpet. He gulped down the eyeball and attached tendons, then screamed in triumph.

One of the EMTs grabbed Astrid's crocheted afghan from the couch and threw it over the parrot to contain him. As he was carried out of the apartment in this makeshift bag, Peaches muttered "Bil-hanā' wa ash-shifā, flachwichser!" to himself again and again.

It took until noon the next day for the New Westminster police to locate Astrid and inform her of her son's passing. They did not share all the details. The president of the Plaza Pointe strata council reached out, too. He picked her up from the ferry terminal and brought her home. By the time Astrid got there, Peaches was in temporary care at the local animal shelter and some of the other strata council members—moved by the tragedy and concerned for Astrid— had cleaned up the worst of accident. But no one was able to get the bloody bird-prints out of the carpet.

She grieved for her dead son, her only child. But her grief was complex. In her secret heart, like many people who love an addict, she was also relieved. *Stan has always gotten himself into trouble, even as a little boy. Maybe it was always going to come to this.*

Astrid was the sole beneficiary in Stan's will. The money earned from the sale of his apartment allowed her to quit her job at Wal-mart. It was enough money to keep Peaches and her in style for the rest of their days. There was even enough money to replace the blood-stained carpet with hardwood flooring.

Best of all, Astrid and Peaches found a new friend in the Arabic-speaking woman who purchased Stan's apartment. The three spent many pleasant sunny afternoons together, sipping mint tea and eating honeyed pastries. Bil-hanā' wa ash-shifā .

Do You Want the Head?

Author's note: *Another pay-the-bills job I have held was that of a technical support agent. The Canadian company I worked for sold technical support services to cable Internet providers in small markets throughout the USA. In other words, small cable companies would hire us to help their residential and commercial customers with any problems they were having with Internet connectivity (rather than setting up their own local call centres). In some locations, cable line installers called us when they needed insight into the status of their install.*

A couple other points to keep in mind: we were not allowed to reveal that we were Canadians. We were required to lie and advise customers that our call centre was in California.

Since I have a strong Canadian accent, that meant I had to tell more lies. Many Americans mis-identify Canadian accents as a "Minnesota" or "Fargo" accents. If I was asked what a nice Minnesota girl like me was doing on the West Coast, I usually said that I had left my small town for the fleshpots of Los Angeles only to find I was far too ugly to break into the movies, and consequently took a tech support job to pay the bills. They usually had nothing more to say after that.

Transcript of <cable support company> Technical Support Call, September 18, 2008.

Chloe: Good morning, you've reached <cable support company>. How can I help?

Line installer: Second tier support for a lineman, please, ma'am.

Chloe: You're in luck, sir, I am a second tier tech. How can I help with your install?

Line installer: Really? A lady on second tier?

Chloe: Last time I checked, sir.

Line installer: Are there any men I can speak with?

Chloe: [as per employer's protocol] Everyone else is on a call, sir. If you prefer, I can take a message and pass it on to the next available male technician.

Line installer: [pauses] Well, I dunno . . .

Chloe: I will try my best to help you, sir, and if I'm awful, you can always request that a man call you back.

Line installer: Ok, I guess I'll just take what I can get.

Author's note: *After that auspicious start, I took the various technical readings he needed, relayed them over the phone, and was able to ping the customer's cable modem. In other words, his installation was successful.*

Line installer: Well, I'm about as pleased as punch with you, young lady.

Author's note: *I was awkwardly arcing into middle age at the time of the call, but I'm told my phone voice sounds 'young', so never mind that.*

Chloe: Glad I could help with your install, sir.

Line installer: Hold on a second, darlin'. You best pull the phone away from your ear.

Chloe: [decreases volume on headset, not knowing what to expect]

Line installer: [sound of shotgun slide loading shells into shotgun, followed by a loud BOOM]

Line installer: [says something muffled]

Chloe: [turns volume up on headset] Sir, are you ok? What's happening?

Line installer: I got that sumbitch, pardon my language, young lady, but I got him.

Chloe: [fearing the worst] Who did you get?

Line installer: That gator.

Chloe: An alligator?

Line installer: He's a devil, that one. If he sees you up a pole, he'll hang around all sneaky-like, hoping you'll come down so's he can take a bite, get him some long-pig. Last month he had me treed up my pole for about an hour, I had to call the office to send someone to scare him away.

Chloe: My goodness, that sounds scary!

Line installer: Aw, t'weren't nothing to it, they just fired buckshot, made a ruckus and he run off. But I've been thinking about him since then. This time I put a string on my shotgun, wore it on my back when I climbed the pole. I was ready for him.

Chloe: So what happens now?

Line installer: Well, Imma climb down and field dress that sucker. There's fancy restaurants that will buy the meat, and leather workers will buy the skin.

Chloe: I see.

Line installer: Yep, they buy it from me right offa that Craig's List. I bet you never seen a gator before.

Chloe: Only on TV.

Line installer: [enthusiastically] I can send you the head, darlin', if you want. Get it stuffed, hang it in your office.

Chloe: Oh, I'm not sure my boss would like that.

Line installer: Well, what he don't know don't hurt him, now does it?

Chloe: [not wanting to offend the line installer by refusing a generous gift, not wanting to get written up by the boss for revealing her location, and fully aware that the decapitated head of an alligator will never make it through Canada customs, Chloe Googles a post office box service in a mid-size California town, gives a made up PO box number and a legit physical address and zip code to the line installer.]

Line installer: Well, you've been mighty gracious, young lady, and I'm happy to send you this head. You tell your boyfriend he don't need to be jealous none, I'm just extending a professional courtesy.

Chloe: Thank you very much. Call again if you need more help.

Line installer: I will, and thank you kindly.

Author's note: *Somewhere there is a postal service company in a mid-size California town with an unclaimed box. Since taxidermy is expensive, I can only assume the line installer sent the gift "wet". Let's hope he had access to one of those nifty vacuum seal machines you can get at Costco.*

Irresistible: A Blood Rain Prequel

Seattle 2014

So far, it had been a typical winter Saturday at Goddess Grove Magickal Emporium. In true Seattle style, the day had started out damp but it was not actually raining. The weak February sun tried valiantly to pierce the patchy cloud cover. Despite that, Star knew that the rain was coming. She didn't need to use her skill with tarot to divine that, though. Her middle-aged knees told her so.

Despite the arthritic ache in her knees, Star was in good humour. Six months ago she had hired a full-time employee to help out around the store.

The young woman in question, Suzanne Murphy, was a sweet, eager person with just a touch of the smart-ass about her. Indeed, in the job interview, when Star asked Suzanne what she thought was one of her weaknesses, Suzanne said, "Well, people tell me that I'm a bit of a smart-ass." Star had raised her eyebrows and asked what did Suzanne think about that? Suzanne had said, "Well, better a smart-ass than a dumb-ass." Star had laughed and hired her on the spot.

Star was pleased with how things were working out. She knew that Suzanne, a recent university graduate, was on a belated gap year. Suzanne had plans to go to graduate school in library science, but—for now, anyway—she was happy working in the Emporium. She was eager to learn all she could about magicks. She coped well with the occasional difficult or demanding customer. That was all good enough for Star, she knew that nothing lasts forever.

As Star sat at the table in the tarot reading alcove, waiting for her noon appointment to show up, she could see that Suzanne had taken the initiative to climb a ladder so she could dust the tops of all the shelves. Suzanne was meticulous, ensuring that books and other items were placed back just so.

Star smiled, and rubbed her aching right knee. She was pleased she didn't have to rehearse every detail of shop-keeping with Suzanne; she also liked that Suzanne kept busy, even when there were no customers in the store. Star could not abide lazy or apathetic people. In her heart of hearts, Star imagined that if she'd ever had a child, perhaps it would have been a daughter like Suzanne.

The bell at the front door tinkled, hopefully announcing the arrival of Star's twelve o'clock. The man who entered was what Star thought of as 'Seattle White Guy 2.0'— average height, average build, brown hair cut short. He was wearing a dark green polar fleece pullover, jeans, and hiking boots that had only ever touched concrete sidewalks.

Suzanne half-turned from her perch on the ladder, looked at the man and asked, "Here for a tarot reading?"

Star noticed the man flick his eyes from Suzanne's hair to her feet, then back again, taking in Suzanne's plus-size body and makeup-less face. He scowled and grunted something Star couldn't quite hear.

Either he's offended by the very idea of tarot or he's another idiot fat-phobe. Star smiled to herself because if this dude was displeased by Suzanne's plumpness, he was really not going to like Star's zaftig physique. Good.

Star herself had long ago worked through the body-shaming certain sexist creeps liked to hand out to random women. As a lesbian feminist witch in a bi-racial relationship who frankly embraced her own fat body, she'd been shamed, yelled at, and generally treated badly by all sorts of assholes. White supremacists had called her a race traitor. Bigoted Christians freaked out about the witchcraft thing or the woman-loving thing. Horny sexists—who seemed to think that every female walked the earth merely to provide aesthetic and sexual pleasure to men—had mocked and ridiculed her. They'd all had a go at Star's self-esteem; none of them had succeeded.

It was at a point now that she thought people with such attitudes were hilarious. At least when she was in certain frames of mind, she secretly enjoyed them making idiotic remarks, because it gave her an opportunity to use the pithy come-backs she had crafted. The bigots were typically not used to getting sass-mouth and laughter as a response. It confused them, which usually made Star laugh all the harder.

Star walked stood up and walked toward the man.

"Are you James, here for a noon reading?"

The man turned from Suzanne, looked Star up and down, and grimaced. Star managed to keep her face blank, impassive, but smiled inwardly.

"No, I'm not James, I'm Chris."

"Not here for a tarot reading?"

"No, I was hoping you sold something like a potion or spell."

"You practice the craft?"

"What craft?" He seemed confused, his eyebrows beetling over the bridge of his nose.

"Ok, sounds like you need a potion," Star said as she walked over to the counter nearest the apothecary armoire.

Suzanne descended the ladder, walked over to the armoire and opened the double doors. Inside were banks of small wooden drawers containing dried herbs, ground minerals, and the other components of potion-craft. Suzanne knew, without being asked, that she would be needed to hand Star the various ingredients of the potion—sous chef readying the ingredients for the master chef.

The man walked up to the potion counter and faced Star. "Why can't I have a spell?" He seemed a little irritated.

"Only practicing witches use spells- there are special skills and knowledge involved in invoking or activating them. If you don't practice witchcraft and know what to do, a spell won't work."

"So teach me then."

Star did not like his tone. She swallowed her irritation. "We do offer some night classes, but it usually takes at least a few months study before a new witch can activate even the simplest of spells."

"Well I don't have time for all that, I need this in less than a week's time!" He was scowling again, like it was Star's fault he didn't know any witchcraft.

Ever the saleswoman, Star nodded sympathetically. "I see, well in that case, I think a potion is really your best option. We compound them here, made to order. Provided we have the ingredients on hand, it's made while you wait. Most commercial potions take about twenty or thirty minutes to brew, stabilize, and bottle. After that, the potion is ready to administer."

'Would I have to use it today?"

"No, if you refrigerate it, it will remain stable for at least ten days, maybe longer, depending on the ingredients."

"Ok," the young man said, talking more to himself than to Star or Suzanne, "today's Saturday the eighth of February, I need it for Friday, February fourteenth, so that should work."

Star's stomach dropped. This was going to turn into a confrontation. Dreading the answer she knew she was going to get, she asked, "Friday February fourteenth? Are you wanting a love potion?"

The man's face lit up. He smirked, the closest thing he had to a smile. "Yes, exactly, a love potion, maybe with a little Spanish Fly in it as well— you know, for the aphrodisiac effect."

Looking over the man's shoulder, Star could see Suzanne's face. She'd grimaced and gone a couple of shades paler as she heard the man's request. Even though Suzanne was still finding her way with magick, she knew what was wrong with such a request.

Star paused, took a breath, and in her best customer service voice said, "Unfortunately, sir, we cannot provide you with such a potion. Is there perhaps a book or set of wind chimes that might interest you instead?"

The man's neck grew red, then his cheeks, then he was red to the hairline. He put his hand on the glass countertop, making the unit creak. "Look, I don't know what the deal is here in your store, I accept that I might not be able to make a spell work on my own without really studying magick, but I'm out of time! I need that potion in time for Valentine's Day."

Over his shoulder, Star could see Suzanne backing away from the customer, edging her way to the portable phone. *She's got good instincts*. They wouldn't be necessary, but Star appreciated the younger woman's caution with this apparently quite volatile man.

"Sir, our store policy is that we don't create or sell love potions."

"Well, why the hell not?" The man drew himself up to his full height, and attempted to loom over Star.

Hard to do with a counter between us, Star thought, *but he's welcome to try*. She suppressed a shrug.

"I can appreciate your eagerness for such a potion; it's just that love potions that actually work— particularly the kind you want, one that also has aphrodisiac qualities . . . they're illegal in every US state."

"Why?!"

"Higher courts have ruled they are the equivalent to giving someone a date-rape drug."

"So?!"

Suzanne caught Star's eye from across the room. She had the portable phone in her hand and a questioning look on her face. Star shook her head. *No need to call the cops*, she thought.

"Giving someone potion that impairs their ability to say no to sex and also forces them to love you is a kind of double assault," Star explained.

The man looked confused.

Star dropped her customer service voice. "Dude, lemme spell it out for you: a potion like that has one purpose and one purpose only: it lets you rape a person's body and her emotions. That's a crime. The Emporium can't be party to that, even if we wanted to." *And boy, do we not want to*, Star thought. Back when Star was young, guys like this used to make her skin crawl, but now she just felt rage. Not a helpful feeling at the moment. She took a deep cleansing breath and forced the muscles in her shoulders to relax.

The man started yelling, exactly what Star did not know, as she was too busy staying grounded and developing her plan. Whatever it was must be pretty awful, though, because Star could see Suzanne's eyes widen in fear. Suzanne actually looked a little green around the gills. Star reckoned that she had let this fella rant long enough. When he stopped long enough to take a quick breath, Star held up her hand in the emblematic "stop" gesture.

"Ok," she said, pretending to capitulate, "Maybe we can compromise. What if I make you a potion— not a love potion you give to someone else, but a potion you drink, to make yourself irresistible?"

"That's not illegal?"

"No, you can drink any potion you want. No law against that."

He thought for a minute.

"And let's say that since we can't provide you with the exact potion you want, an irresistibility potion would be . . . say . . . fifty per cent off?" Star looked at him shrewdly.

He thought some more. Eventually, he said, "Ok, I can work with that. When can it be ready?"

"Irresistibility potions don't take long, should be only about fifteen minutes. There's a coffee house across the street, they give us free drink coupons. May I offer you one by way of apology for your troubles today?"

"Sure," he said, snatching the offered coupon from Star's hand. "I'll be back in fifteen." He stalked out of the Emporium and jaywalked across the street to the coffee shop.

Suzanne came to stand near Star. Her eyes were as round as an owl's, and her eyebrows raised to maximum incredulity. "Good grief! I thought I was gonna have to call 9-1-1."

"Not to worry, Suzanne, I got this."

"I don't see how making that guy irresistible is much better than what he wanted to start with," Suzanne said reproachfully.

Star grinned. "I didn't say I was going to make him irresistible to women."

Suzanne's eyes got even rounder. "So you're going to make him irresistible to men?"

"Nope. Now, let's get started, we're going to need a few things from the armoire, and the lint brush outta my purse."

Suzanne gathered the items as required. Working together over the Bunsen burner, they crafted the potion in only ten minutes, and Suzanne went into the storage room in back to continue her dusting and tidying.

Star returned to her seat in the tarot reading alcove. *Where is that twelve noon appointment? I think I'm gonna have to implement a deposit system or something. Too many no-shows lately.*

The potion was still cooling when the man returned from the coffee shop, take-out cup in hand.

"Will it taste bad?" he asked Star as he threw two twenty dollar bills down on the counter.

"Yes, most certainly."

"Can I just pour it in my latte and take it that way?"

"It doesn't matter if you mix it with food or drink, but don't consume it until it is room temperature," Star cautioned.

"Why?"

"You might burn the roof of your mouth. Have a nice day, sir, and thank you for shopping at Green Goddess Magickal Emporium."

He left the store without another word.

The next Saturday, the man was waiting outside the Emporium when Star arrived to unlock the door. He was surrounded by dozens of cats: big muscular toms with tattered ears lolling on the ground; fuzzy half-grown ginger kittens scaling his pants legs with their tiny needle claws; sedate tabbies with loud purrs; mischievous Tuxedo cats trying to find a place from which they could jump to settle on his shoulders; long-tailed Siamese looking up at him with adoration in their slightly crossed eyes.

When the man saw Star, he started to screech. "You bitch! You bitch! Look at what you've done! Get these damn things offa me!"

Star smiled sweetly, and leaned over to scritch one of the tabbies behind the ears. The tabby purred more loudly. Looking at up Chris while she stroked the silky fur of one of the toms, Star smiled.

"Sir, whatever do you mean?"

His face was blotchy from frustration, and a vein in his forehead throbbed. "These cats! You did this! Fix it, you fucking bitch!"

Star stood up, pulled her keys from her purse, and unlocked the Emporium door. Over her shoulder, she looked the man. "I don't understand; you said you wanted to be irresistible. I made you a potion for that. Clearly it worked. What's the problem?"

"I didn't want to be irresistible to fucking CATS! I wanted to be irresistible to women, for Christ's sake."

Star turned to face him. "No need to go bring Him into the conversation, sir. If you wanted a more specific potion, you really should have indicated. However, there is a way to undo the workings of the potion."

"Anything! Please! Just do it! I fucking can't stand cats."

Star looked around at the animals. "Oh, don't say that, you'll hurt their feelings." She scooped the largest of the Tuxedo cats up into her arms. "If you're that certain you don't want their adoration, come in, I can fix it . . . for a price."

"Argh. Of course. Fuck," he glowered.

"It's a limited time offer," she said, walking across the Emporium's threshold. "You darlings are invited in as well. Cats are always welcome in the Emporium."

The animals perked up their ears, and ran inside, except for the regal Tuxedo cat in Star's arms. He allowed himself to be carried over the threshold, then leapt lightly from her arms to the nearest window sill. He started to lick a paw and use it to wash his face.

"Perhaps you all need a bath," she suggested to the felines. All the cats sat and started to groom themselves.

"As for you," Star said to the man as he crossed the threshold, "you sit yourself down in the tarot alcove and wait. It will take me a while to work the right spell to undo irresistibility, at least an hour. Should cost, hhm, let's see, a hundred bucks."

The man grimaced, and his eyes burned with hatred, but he nodded.

"Up front, if you please."

He pulled five twenties from his wallet, slapped them on the counter, and then sat in the tarot alcove without another word.

* * *

Star was just whispering the magickal "get yourself home safely" instructions to the last three or four cats when Suzanne arrived for her two pm shift. The effects of potion had been undone a couple of hours before. The man had exited quietly, but Star wanted to be sure that none of the kitties came to any harm after their experience.

Suzanne looked around and shivered.

"Feeling the magic I used to ward the Emporium?" Star asked.

"Yes, as soon as I stepped over the threshold I felt it."

"What does it feel like to you?"

"It tickles."

Star smiled at the younger woman. "That's because you have no evil intent. If you did, you'd end up feeling tired, exhausted really, too tired to speak or argue."

"How many cats were drawn to him?"

"A few dozen. He hated it."

"I'm glad he may have learned his lesson, but this worries me," Suzanne said

"Really? What part?"

"The three-fold rule."

"What about it?"

"Well, you tricked the guy, and made him miserable for a day or so . . . doesn't that come back on you three-fold? Suzanne asked

Star plugged in the kettle and readied the supplies for tea.

"I didn't trick him, he had evil intentions and he was not specific. I myself think it would be lovely, if a bit inconvenient, to be irresistible to cats. So if somehow Karma in her wisdom gives me three days of intense cat-love, I am perfectly ok with that. It's a small sacrifice to keep him from assaulting some poor woman."

Suzanne thought about it for a moment. "Well, I guess if you're willing to do the time without whining, I'm ok with you doing the crime." She made air quotes with her fingers for the word "crime."

"Meanwhile, it's a good reminder to me to keep the wards around the shop in tip-top shape. I think they must have gotten loose and flabby if he was able to cross the threshold in the first place. That's the karmic debt I'm worried about."

"It seems like you already strengthened them."

"Yes, last night after the astral projection class was finished, I did a bit of work on them, but they need more."

"I'd like to help you with that; I think it would be good practice for me."

Star nodded. "Good idea! The water's boiled, so let's have some tea before we start."

Bettina's Birthday

More than anything, Bettina, age eleven, wanted a birthday cake baked by her mother. She found ways to trick herself into believing this was possible. But on some level, she knew she was never going to get that cake. Bettina's mother had died giving birth to her. They had not even had a chance to meet.

Bettina hated telling people that part. She felt degraded by the pity she saw on their faces. No one at her new school knew about her motherless existence. Bettina and her dad Phillip had just moved to Brampton in late August. Teachers and kids made assumptions about Bettina's home life. "Does your mom travel for her work?" "Are your parents divorced?" Bettina would shrug and allow them to believe whatever they had invented.

When Bettina was away from school—taking the bus by herself, for example, or playing in the park with unfamiliar children in other neighbourhoods—on those occasions, Bettina could step out of her sorrow. "My mom is picking me up later, after she is finished at her veterinary job" was a favourite conversation starter. The other children listened intensely to Bettina's detailed stories. Her mother was nursing a sick tiger back to health at a zoo. Her mother had discovered an injured and filthy fledgling crow, brought it home, and taught it to say words like a parrot.

Bettina had repeated the stories so often, they felt more like memories than fabrications. And that was how Bettina found herself inviting six or seven unfamiliar playground kids to her birthday party.

As one part of her mind recoiled in horror at the implication, another part just kept on talking. Somehow she couldn't stop herself. Her heart pounded so fast she imagined it might burst from her chest. Nevertheless, she boasted that her mother made the most delicious confetti cake in the world, and that she was baking just such a cake, in the shape of a rainbow glitter unicorn, for Bettina's twelfth birthday party.

When Bettina went home that night, she told her father that she wanted to have a birthday party the following Saturday. Bettina's dad, Phillip, was pleased. He took this as a sign Bettina was coming out of her shell, making friends at her new school. Bettina had never asked to have a party before. Phillip was happy to host one, buy a cake, and hang streamers on short notice. He knew nothing about Bettina's excursions to playgrounds far from home. He knew nothing about her lies.

Bettina considered telling him what had happened at the playground, but stopped herself. Whenever she mentioned her mom to her dad, his eyes got sad, even if his face was smiling. She couldn't bear seeing that look on his face.

When the day and hour of the party arrived, the guests started to trickle in. Some kids were dropped off out in front of the house, parents speeding away in eager anticipation of child-free time. Other kids arrived with their parents in tow, hovering, clearly concerned about what sort of child-eating monsters had planned this party.

Bettina's dad led the hover-parents into the kitchen, and plied them with drinks and food. Bettina and the seven playground kids stood in the living room.

"Where's your mom?" asked Mercedes, the tallest of the playground kids. "I am so excited to meet her. I think maybe I want to be a vet when I grow up."

"Yeah, where's your mom? Where's the crow?" asked Emma, Mercedes' best friend.

"Ah, there was . . . um . . . a problem this morning," Bettina said, making it up as she went along. "A dog got hit by a car, so . . . she had to go into work . . . to operate on him."

"What kind of dog?" asked Jeremy, the quietest of the boys. "Not a German Shepherd! I have a German Shepherd." His cheeks grew pink, and his eyes round.

"Oh don't worry," said Jeremy's older sister, Caitlyn. "Chester was in the yard when we left home, he was fine! I do want to see your crow, though. Maybe we can teach him a swear word!" she giggled.

The kids laughed, except Bettina.

"We should teach him the word "fart"!" suggested Max.

Alice and Patrick and Max laughed, but Caitlyn and Mercedes scowled. Emma started to giggle, too, but stopped when she saw Mercedes was not laughing.

"'Fart' is not a swear," declared Emma, looking at Mercedes for approval.

Mercedes nodded. "You're just a baby, Max, what do you know about swearing?"

"I know 'shit' and 'damn'." Max drew himself to his full height and squared his shoulders.

"I think we should see this crow before we decide what word to teach him," Alice said. "Maybe he's not a swearing kind of crow."

"We want the crow! We want the crow! We want the crow!" chanted the playground kids.

"Er, um he's resting right now, um, he's a nocturnal kind of crow." Bettina felt her face flame, and she stared at the carpet. "Maybe we could play a board game? Or watch a video?"

"We want the crow. We want the crow. Wake him up, wake him up!"

"What's this?" said Bettina's dad, poking his head around the corner. "What is it that you guys want?"

Bettina could see the faces of the other parents standing behind her dad, also peering into the living room.

Before Bettina could think of what to say, Mercedes said, "We've heard so much about Bettina's mom, we wanted to meet her, because I want to be a vet one day."

Bettina's dad's eyebrows shot up to his hairline.

"Then Bettina said she was called in to work because the German Shepherd needed surgery after his car accident", added Jeremy, "But it wasn't my German Shepherd who was hurt. Chester is ok."

"Of course he is, dummy," Caitlyn said to her brother. "I told you Chester is at home and he's fine."

Bettina's dad's face went white, and the parents behind him started to whisper among themselves. Bettina wished she could crawl under the couch and die. She felt tears well up in her eyes, and tried to blink them away.

Mercedes observed Bettina carefully. Fixing her eyes on her, Mercedes addressed the adults in a voice as sweet as golden syrup. "But if we can't meet Bettina's mom, then at least we want to meet the crow she taught to how to talk."

Everyone started to talk all at once, voices angry. Soon the adults were shouting.

Jeremy and Max started to cry, and Alice tried to comfort them. Emma sidled up to Mercedes and whispered in her ear, and poor Caitlyn held very still, trying to manage her panic.

Mercedes stepped close to Bettina and whispered, "I always knew you were lying. Now everyone else knows, too! "

"Yeah," said Emma, "and crows aren't nocturnal, everybody knows that!"

Mercedes and Emma retreated to one corner of the living room and continued to whisper while they gave Bettina the stink-eye.

Bettina felt hollow in the pit of her stomach. Her whole body flushed. Her cheeks were burning. She wanted to say something really mean to Mercedes and Emma, but couldn't, because her mouth had gone dry. It was like her tongue was soldered to the roof of her mouth.

She ran out of the living room, up the stairs, and into her bedroom, slamming the door behind her. She threw herself headlong onto her bed, wracked with silent sobs. She didn't want anyone to know she was crying. There was so much commotion downstairs, Bettina could have wailed and not been heard.

An hour later, the house quiet as the grave, Phillip knocked on her door.

"Bet?"

"What?" Bettina's nose was stuffed up from crying, and her face was blotchy.

"Can we talk about what . . . that all . . . was today?"

"No!"

"Bet, please? I'm worried . . ."

"I said NO!" Bettina buried her face in her pillow and started to sob some more.

Phillip stood helplessly in her doorway. When little Bettina had been upset, he had known what to do.

He used to sweep her into his arms, hugging her, rocking her angry toddler body until he felt her muscles relax. Once she relaxed, he could always make her giggle by tossing her in the air, or blowing a zerbert on her bare tummy.

Faced with angry, ashamed 'tween Bettina, he was at a loss.

He knew that to treat her like the baby she'd been would offend her dignity. He had long hoped that she—having never known a mother—wouldn't miss what she'd never had. Clearly, he had been wrong.

He felt like a big dope. After a few minutes, Bettina's dad backed out of the doorway and quietly closed her bedroom door.

To Bettina's great relief, they did not discuss it that evening. They simply sat on the couch, ate leftover snacks from the ruined party, and watched a documentary about penguins.

Right as the show was ending, the doorbell rang.

When Phillip opened the door, there was no one there.

"Hey, come look at this!" he called to Bettina.

Bettina went into the hall and stood next to her father.

On the porch there was a small stuffed unicorn toy, fashioned to sit upright. Between his stuffed pink hooves, pressed against his stuffed round belly, there was a small pink cardboard box.

"Go ahead, open it, it must be for you, since it's your birthday."

Bettina knelt on the porch and opened the pink box. Her dad crouched down next to her to look, too.

Inside the box was a confetti cupcake, loaded with swirls and swirls of pink and purple icing, topped with rainbow sprinkles. Bettina carefully lifted the cupcake from the box and noticed there was a folded slip of paper at the bottom. Handing the cupcake to her dad, Bettina unfolded the paper.

On it, written with a pink glitter pen, was the message: YOU WILL BE LOVED. There was no signature.

About the Author

Chloe Cocking writes books, which should not surprise you, considering you are reading this. A committed caffeine enthusiast, she has never met a cup of coffee she didn't like.

Photo Credit: Robert Cocking

Ms. Cocking writes urban fantasy, humour, fables and fairy tales, and whatever else captures her fancy. She enjoys pie, as should all right-thinking people.

Her first novel, *Blood Rain*, was published in 2017 by Filidh Publishing. She lives in New Westminster with another human and two cats, one of whom frequently masquerades as a small angry sweater

You can check out more of her shennanagins on her website http://chloecocking.com